# HUMAN
# STORIES

## 16 TALES OF THE AFFLICTED MIND

HENRY O'CONNELL
FRANK MCKENNA
KEVIN LALLY

# Contents

# ACKNOWLEDGEMENTS

*Thank you, Alison, for knowing that, sometimes, my head likes to be in the clouds. And for reminding me that life is in the moments.*

~Frank

*Thanks, as always, to Kathy.*

~Henry

*To Fiona, when everything else was falling apart, you kept us whole.*

~Kevin

# MEMORIES

Frank McKenna

Charlie Summers stands in front of his sitting-room window, forehead resting on the triple-glaze. The Shannon Bridge stretches out beneath him, the Shannon itself rushing from right to left the entire width of his view. On the television, the Taoiseach congratulates him and the rest of the nation on their obedience and begins to deliver the news Charlie's neighbour, John, predicted he would.

Well, what John actually said was, *That fucker Varadkar will drag this bullshit out 'til the end of the year*, but the gist aligned.

Measures are to be intensified and time-periods extended, indefinitely. Charlie can now travel no farther than two kilometres from home. He wonders if, in the years since he was brought to this apartment, he has ever been more than two kilometres from home.

Now Taoiseach Varadkar is sharing heart-warming stories of compassionate acts performed during restrictions. He talks about letters he received, letters that thank *him,* personally. He uses the first names of those who penned the letters. He does not say how old these people are, but their words are innocent, and Charlie thinks they must be children. The Taoiseach is explaining how the letters give him hope: he *knows* the Irish nation will be okay because of what the letters contain. Charlie hopes he is right.

"We must come together by remaining apart," the Taoiseach says.

As long as he has been living there, Charlie has spent much of his time looking out over the Shannon Bridge's long, subtle arch. He watches cars entering and leaving Limerick City. He observes the flags that hang from the streetlights, punctuating each side of the bridge and how they change with the seasons; Limerick flags in GAA season, Munster flags in rugby season. It was the rainbow flag during the Gay Marriage Referendum. Now there are no flags. Covid season. He watches the cyclists, the walkers, the runners and all their different paces and animations. In particular, he watches Jenny Thomas.

The very first day he arrived – the first day he looked out at that view – there she was. What grabbed his attention, tweaked his recognition, was her wavy red hair gathered high through a thick white bobbin, bouncing as she strode. He had blinked and pressed against the glass, disbelieving, desperate to be sure. Every morning, she bobs across the bridge, over the flowing water, in his direction. So, he rises early, waits until she appears at the far side and observes her crossing, sharpening into glorious clarity, before she passes beneath him and into the city.

He palms his phone in his hand. *She won't have posted. She'll be watching, like me. Like everyone else.*

After the ad break, the pundits talk about the speech. *It's good to have things confirmed. Varadkar is doing well. Ireland is doing well. The important thing is not to get complacent, to keep digging in, isolating.*

Isolating.

Charlie turns off the TV and steps out of his apartment. John's door is across the hallway. Charlie imagines the clunking sound of it unlocking from the inside and John peering out from his dark apartment. John's apartment always looks dark from the outside. *What do you make of it?* John would ask, thrusting a finger over Charlie's shoulder at the TV.

Charlie had recently taken to using the stairs – six floors down, six floors up – because the buckle of his belt had been pinching the underside of his belly. This is something he is particularly aware of, as the doctors ask about it continually. *How is your appetite? Have you noticed your clothes being a little tighter?*

But today does not seem like a normal day, so he takes the elevator.

It feels strange to be on the street. There is nobody on the footpath in either direction. He cannot see, or even hear, any cars or trucks or motorbikes. The Shannon Bridge is empty.

He walks up the hill towards Henry Street to the shop on the corner. The doors open when he steps in front of them. An older woman is approaching from inside and stops when she sees him. They stand on either side of the doorway. He thinks to step aside to let her pass, but she has already retreated into the shop and moved into the corner. She turns her face away. He hurries in but pauses for a moment. He had hoped to get a Coke, but the woman is standing in front of the soft drinks. She shuffles her feet and looks from side to side – anywhere but straight at him. He decides not to get the Coke and moves further into the shop. The woman scurries out behind him.

Two big, yellow signs rise from the floor just inside the door, but Charlie had rushed past and not read them. There are yellow stickers on the floor saying to keep a two-metre distance from other people and similar stickers on the counter where he places his items.

"Hi, Pavel," he says to the teller through a sheet of plastic glass. "I'm Charlie." He has read Pavel's nametag many times but has never before felt compelled to use it.

"Hi, Charlie."

Pavel does not smile. He raises his eyebrows when Charlie asks for two bags to separate his items. He full-on scowls when Charlie tries to hand him money under the plastic glass rather than use a card. At least he looks at Charlie, though, not like the woman at the front of the shop.

When he gets back to his apartment, Charlie writes a short note and leaves it in front of John's door. He places one of his shopping bags on top of it. He thinks of knocking, of seeing John's smiling and grateful face. He imagines John inviting him in for tea or coffee or a beer, but he knows, with Covid and social distancing, he could not go in. So, he doesn't knock, and he returns to his apartment, feeling sorry that John, being on the other side of the corridor, probably has no view of the river.

When an alarm sounds on Charlie's phone, he pours a glass of water from the kitchen sink. He moves to the living area and slides out the drawer under the coffee table, from which he removes two items: a blister pack of pills and a white souvenir thimble. He rolls the thimble gently between his fingers, feeling its delicate smoothness, and considers its simple depiction of a windmill with green grass and a blue sky. Beneath the picture is a single word: Lyon. He pierces the film over the blister pack's Thursday afternoon pot and spills its two pills onto his hand. He chases the small one down his throat with a sip of water, then the big pill with two big gulps. They leave a dry taste. Through the window, he sees a small, silver car passing slowly over the bridge, leaving the city.

Moments later, Jenny Thomas is glowing out from the screen on Charlie's phone. "So, there we have it," she says. He thinks she used to have more freckles bridging her nose, clustered on her cheeks, but he can't be sure.

"No end in sight yet," she says, smiling. She smiles at him every day. She tells him positive things every day. She tells him to keep exploring and tells him how good she feels after her run through the park and over the river and through the city. "You've been amazing," she says, looking directly at him. "I don't know what I'd do without you."

Jenny's eyes glisten over her last words. She blinks, and the glisten is gone, then her Insta-story ends. Charlie frowns. He returns to the start of the story and watches it again, a creeping unease in his chest.

He flicks through Jenny's previous posts, through all the positive thoughts and messages she shares with Charlie and everyone else.

He dwells on a particular video, which begins by focusing on what looks like a tea-cake stand. Jenny lifts a glass dome to uncover three tiers, not of miniature cakes but of thimbles. One by one, she presents each thimble to the camera and identifies the destination from where it was acquired. "Each is a memory," she explains. The thimble from Mexico brought back to her the image of a turquoise sea, of rugged, vibrant-green hills, and an aroma of street-stall quesadillas. The one from Las Vegas did not remind her of luminous casinos and desert heat, but of how her first views of the Grand Canyon, through a thinning layer of trees on the approaching road, had been like glimpsing "fragments of an unfathomable, otherworldly beast." Charlie watches the video as he has before, countless times, scanning each of Jenny's thimbles with the dread that he would suddenly realise that one bore the word *Lyon*.

He startles as someone thumps on his door.

"What's this about?" demands John, taking an exaggerated step back from Charlie, holding up the bag of groceries Charlie had left at his door.

"They're for you." Charlie offers a smile. "Because of Covid."

"You think I can't go to the shop?"

Charlie's shoulders curl over a little, and his eyes drop from John's face to the bag in John's hand. "I'm sorry, I just thought…."

John tosses the bag at Charlie's feet. A tin of beans rolls out, clunking against the wall. "I don't suppose you sanitised your hands before you left it at my door?"

Charlie gathers the groceries into the bag and returns to his apartment. He wonders if he should apologise again to John for all that trouble with the Gardaí the last time he was sick.

He shakes himself, shooing away the memories of that time. The thoughts and atmosphere around them, they stalk him, waiting for a loosening, an unclenching, so they can seep back in. He finds his thimble and grips it in his palm. He tries to sink back into the moment, before which everything had been an ambitious climb, from which the entire world seemed visible and accessible, after which everything fell apart. The moment he was kissed by Jenny Thomas.

At some random final-days-of-college party, in a house shortly to be returned to its owner, Charlie had found himself sharing a couch with the freckled, red-haired girl that he had often seen bouncing around campus. That night, she wore a daisy in her hair, just above her ear – and, somehow, this did not seem strange. She was telling him about her small collection of thimbles – one from each of the four countries she had visited – and how she would spend the years to come filling the wall of her bedroom with these mementoes of her explorations.

"The best thing about them," she said, leaning in, "is that nobody notices them. But they're in every airport." She smiled widely, toothily, eyes lit up by his interest. And Charlie found himself vowing that, from his upcoming adventure summering in southern France, he would return with the first of his own collection.

Later that evening, Jenny Thomas swept by him as he sat alone. It may have been the drink, or the euphoria of the last days of college, or the overwhelming sense of possibility, but she traced her hand across the line of his shoulders and brought a palm to rest on his cheek. She lowered her face as though she had done it a thousand times and softly pressed her lips to his.

Before she danced away, she held there long enough for him to capture what flamed his hope through years of being unable to keep hold of himself—a moment of exhilaration and boundless promise.

He squeezes the thimble tighter, trying to force himself back there. It used to only take a thought, and he would feel again that jolt of surprise as her lips touched his, the sense of marvel at the clarity of her skin and the innocence of her freckles, at the daisy in her hair. He used to allow it to lift him from reality or maybe bring him back to reality. It was his portal. But time has done its work. Now, the texture is gone. Her face, the taste, the scent, the sounds in the room have all become less tangible, like a dream fading as wakefulness returns. It distresses him that such a memory could reduce to so little, and he clings to his single thimble, lest it disappear completely.

A notification appears on his screen—a new story.

"I'm sorry," are Jenny's first words, and tears slide down both cheeks. Charlie sits up in his chair and stares into the screen, his jaw clenching. "I felt I should be honest with you. I thought I was managing, but with these new restrictions and everything I've been reading and listening to…it feels like there's no end to it. I'm feeling…like the world is closing in."

Charlie stands when the post ends, gazing out over the bridge. The thimble is a solid nugget in the centre of his clenched fist.

*

Some time ago, Charlie began piecing together where

Jenny lived. It wasn't a conscious thing. Little clues caught his attention and organised in his mind. Posts would show her walking by the University Maternity Hospital. Many posts were from Shelbourne Park, just around the corner from the hospital. She ran from that direction over the Shannon Bridge. Then one day, she posted a story of herself opening a letter – an invitation to some blogger's party in Dublin – and there was her address right on the envelope. It was visible for less than a second. Charlie had to pause the story to read it, but he made it out and wrote it down. He worried the wrong kind of person might see it and know where she lived.

Glenview Gardens is outside Charlie's two-kilometre radius, but he feels no guilt. The area is greyer than he imagined. Jenny always seems to be surrounded by grass and trees or, before lockdown, the sea. When he sees her run, she is running over the river. To him, she is nature.

*

His summer adventure in France had not been as he imagined. At night, he had lain for hours in bed, his chest tightening, his breath quickening. After slipping, finally, to sleep, he would wake after three hours, then two, then after only minutes.

He was tormented by that night with Jenny Thomas – that a single kiss was where they had ended. By being too timid to make contact before he left, he had betrayed the purity of that moment.

Days became minefields where his companions were threats and strangers sought him out. He was tainted. And people could *tell*. He saw it in the looks they gave him, in the looks they did not. He heard it in what they said and in what they did not. He holed himself away because everything was closing in. He could feel the constriction.

He heard them from his room. They called him *Coward*. They called him *Traitor*. And when the tapping started on the door and soft voices tried to coax him out, he knew what was in store, so he hid deeper. But the voices became louder. The tapping became pounding. They pounded and pounded, and then, eventually, as he knew they would, they broke through the door and took him.

*Committed*, his parents had said. *To keep you safe.*

He had not been able to argue against his capture. Something had gone very wrong. Whatever it was is not wrong now, but it exists inside him somewhere, waiting.

\*

In Glenview Gardens, Jenny's house is at the end of the terrace. He walks along the alley by its side and is able to see over the wall into her small, concrete back garden. A line of clay pots with colourful flowers runs along the inside perimeter. Some of the flowers are familiar to him – the subjects of previous stories – but they do not seem as interesting as they did when Jenny was narrating their addition to her collection, pointing out their unique features.

Charlie has seen the full-height windows at the back of Jenny's house many times from the inside of her open-plan kitchen-living room. He tries to look through the glass but sees only darkness. He thinks about calling at her front door and watching for recognition on her face. He thinks about apologising for never contacting her but then wonders if she would even remember a kiss with a boy that came and went a long time ago.

He needs to see her. To see that she is okay. That she is still *there*.

He tells himself the story of that night, but he cannot *feel* it anymore. He cannot *return* there anymore.

He shakes his head. Shakes his whole body.

He walks around to the front of the house and stands in the centre of her open gate. Memory is what he held onto when his freedom was taken. Memory is where he went when they told him he was getting better and told him in the same breath that he would never be the same again. It was where he continued to go every dreary day between every caving-in of his world. Then one day, after another restart, there she was, bounding towards him across the bridge – a growing spec that told him a memory was not all this world had left in store for him. He had found her on his phone, and she was in his life again, smiling right at him, telling him to keep going, to keep exploring.

*

Jenny Thomas has spent the last thirty minutes in the darkness of her sitting room, flicking through the dozens of direct messages landing in her Instagram account. It is the biggest and quickest reaction to anything she has ever posted. She feels relief. *People are listening.*

She jumps when her doorbell rings. It has been a long time since anyone but the postman has rung that bell. A hope rises, but she thinks it foolish to imagine her video would inspire anyone to offer their company.

*Of course*, she thinks, after opening the door to the empty night. *A joke. Kids playing a prank.* She stares into the driveway and feels herself sink, tears returning to her eyes.

But as she moves to close the door, the light catches on something pristine and glossy white on the welcome mat at her feet.

There is no one on the pavement. The road is clear, and she hears no sounds, even in the distance, of cars or trucks or motorbikes.

She bends down and picks up the thimble, just like the thirty-seven she has in the tea-cake display case in her bedroom. It is not one she has seen before. The image is of a windmill and the place name inked in simple handwriting-style is of a town in the south of France where she has never been.

She holds it and feels the slightest shift inside her.

Distant and familiar. She looks deeper into the shadowed spaces where the streetlights don't quite reach and wonders if she can see something move.

# Six Months at Fort Apache

Henry O'Connell

## July 1st, 1998

First day down. Kelly and myself just did our first day as SHOs in A&E. Big boys now. No longer interns. The A&E is smaller than I thought it would be and doesn't seem too busy. A few nice-looking nurses. We went straight back to the flat after the shift and tried to be mature for a while by reading textbooks, but then we caved and went for pints. Now I'm writing a bloody diary. (I hope Kelly never finds this, or he'll think I'm gone soft.) I want to keep a record of the next six months. Maybe if I write things down as I see them, I can start to learn and become a half-decent doctor. My internship was so bloody chaotic – so much drinking and partying – I really don't think I learned anything. I just survived. This year will be different.

## July 8th

The new registrar arrives, a week late. *Total* ride.

Blonde, posh, from Cork. Her name is Susan Sheridan – Kelly and I already call her 'Sexy Sue'. Must be careful with that. Apparently, she had problems in her last post and left, came out here to the wilds of the west of Ireland. Must be some story. The nurses will get it out of her. I must ask Margaret. She's the nicest of the nurses.

## July 10th

Not sure if I'm learning much yet, but maybe there isn't much to learn. Kelly and I had a quietish day. Mainly sprains, cuts and bruises, and two RTIs. They probably could all have gone to their GP. Sexy Sue watches everything we do, like she thinks we're idiots. Which we are.

## July 12th

Kelly and I have our first night out with the nurses. Good craic! We get fairly hammered in the town and then go back to one of their houses for a party. By the end, there was just Kelly, me, Margaret and Jane. Kelly took Jane, and I took Margaret. Strike one for the boys.

## July 14th

It's Bastille Day, so Kelly and I spend the whole day talking to the nurses in French accents. They think it's funny, at first. Sexy Sue doesn't seem to get it.

## July 18th

I have trouble getting a line in on an elderly, dehydrated patient. I have to get help from Sexy Sue. She smiles at me as she put in the line – she has an odd smile. Either she feels sorry for me, or she fancies me. We must get the nurses to get her out with us some night. I ask Margaret if she can arrange something. She doesn't seem happy, as I think she's into me after our night of passion together.

## July 21st

Kelly and I have decided that this place is wilder than we thought. The locals are nice, but they don't seem to follow basic rules of civilization, like only driving when you're sober. Loads of drink drivers come through, sometimes with questions from the Gardaí after. And on Sunday evenings, we've started to notice the pattern of hurlers coming in after matches to be stitched up.

## July 22nd

Because of the wild nature of the locals, we've decided to call the A&E 'Fort Apache', after that Paul Newman film *Fort Apache the Bronx*. Newman and his buddies were cool policemen under siege from the public. We're cool doctors under siege from wild culchies. I make a point of trying to look and sound like Paul Newman, swanning around A&E today.

Kelly notices and starts laughing uncontrollably.

## July 24th

So, there's a consultant! Margaret told me that there's supposed to be an A&E consultant for Fort Apache. And he's on duty all the time. It's now nearly August, and I've never seen him set foot in the place. Occasionally, he rings in and talks to one of the senior nurses. He does private practice in the town, mainly medicolegal reports. O'Keeffe is his name. Kelly and I put up a chart on the wall in the res with 'Days without consultant entering Fort Apache' and write in '24'.

## July 25th

The res is okay, by the way. The usual. Small television, toaster, manky bedrooms. At least we can smoke here with ease – no smoke alarms. There's a small room off Fort Apache where we go for smokes when we're very busy and can't get back to the res. But it's a pain smoking there because the room has a smoke alarm. We have to stretch a rubber glove around it to stop it from going off.

## August 1st

Margaret has a house party and starts acting like my girlfriend. Oh no. She was just supposed to arrange something so we could invite Sexy Sue. Sexy Sue seems to spend her whole time at Fort Apache and said she was too busy to come to the party. I get very drunk and spend the night with Margaret again. I may be giving her the wrong message now. Kelly beds one of the student nurses and then spends the whole next day telling me how he can't STAND her.

## August 10th

The surgical registrar is a total slob, and we HATE him. We call him to look at the odd X-ray for fractures or for acute abdomens. He *actually* smells. He's fat, bald, and a big bully, essentially. Kelly and I watched him today as he was looking at an ankle X-ray we'd given him. As he looked at it, he yawned, frowned, PICKED HIS NOSE and scratched his arse. Then he tried to convince us there was no fracture. In the end, we got Mary, the nurse in charge, to talk to him. He went off with a big red face and shouted at me to send the 'fucking patient' up to surgical.

## August 15th

I still don't know what I want to do. Kelly's the same. That's why we're doing this six-month job in Fort Apache. Because of that surgical slob, (the registrar who can't read x-rays,) I don't want to do surgery. Sexy Sue seems to want to be a renal physician or something fancy. But I couldn't be like her. She's here before us for every shift and always last to leave. No wonder her wedding was cancelled. (The nurses got that information out of her.) Kelly has mixed emotions on hearing the news – sorry she's had a serious boyfriend, but happy she's single.

## August 22nd

Margaret has started calling me 'honey', even at Fort Apache. Maybe I should just stick with her until Christmas and then break up with her when I move on to my next job in January. She'll go mental if I dump her now. And the other nurses would probably kill me, too. Except maybe Jenny. I think she fancies me.

## September 5th

Psychiatry. *That's* what I want to do. I had to get a psychiatry consult today on a young woman who took an overdose. It was a busy evening, bodies and trolleys everywhere. In swanned the psychiatrist, cool as you like. No white coat for him. He was wearing a nice check shirt and navy corduroys, and he carried a leather-bound notebook. As I rattled off the details on the patient, he just smiled at me patiently. Then he spent an hour with the patient. AN HOUR. I timed him! He wrote a note on the chart and came back to me when he was done, smiling. 'She's fine. You can let her off. I'll see her in the clinic next week'. Cool dude. Psychiatry it is. Kelly wants to do renal medicine because he's in love with Sexy Sue.

## September 12th

Kelly asks Sexy Sue out, and she starts screaming at him. Holy shit.

## September 15th

Margaret said she'd like me to meet her parents. This is getting out of control. How can I string her along for another three months???

## October 10th

The nurse in charge approaches Kelly and me with a worried look this evening. I knew we'd mess up. I was already thinking up excuses before she opened her mouth. I think of the chart in the res on days since the consultant set foot in Fort Apache – it now says 102. He's NEVER been here in our time. So how can we be blamed for anything that's gone wrong in this place? Sexy Sue is always too busy to ask for help. The surgical reg is a slob who won't accept anything for admission to his ward. The medical reg is nearly as bad. But when she sat us down, all she wanted to talk about was Sexy Sue. She's worried about her. "I'm very worried about Dr Sheridan," she says. (Sexy Sue, she means.) I'm relieved. She goes on about Sue being snappy with the nurses and refusing to go home after shifts, yet never being able to get through her work.

I'm so relieved she doesn't have a complaint about me or Kelly that I don't really listen to her. Kelly says on the way home that Sexy Sue being stressed might be a chance for him to get in with her. We laugh at that one. I call Margaret, and we have a party with the nurses to celebrate our relief that we're not in trouble.

## October 28th

Kelly and I are actually getting a bit worried about Sexy Sue now. I've noticed she doesn't ever change her clothes. She used to be so stylish. She looks worn out. Even Kelly has gone off her. The nurses are still worried, so I tell them to call the consultant, O'Keeffe. Of course, they don't dare.

## November 8th

So now I'm studying for the psychiatry membership exams. That cool dude psychiatrist has inspired me. I want to be in a speciality where you have the luxury of spending an hour talking with your patient. Or maybe that's just him.

## November 11th

I'm reading lots of basic psychology, psychopharmacology, and psychopathology for the Psychiatry Membership Exams. Kelly still doesn't know what he wants to do. He's half afraid of Sexy Sue now, as she gives him daggers looks whenever she sees him. And he's doing a fairly steady line with the student nurse he hates.

## November 25th

Sexy Sue looked wretched today. The nurses are worried. Even Kelly and I are worried at this stage. She can't seem to handle any kind of stress now. Still no sign of O'Keeffe. That's 149 days.

## December 2nd

I'm nearly there with the Margaret situation. Avoided meeting the family, and I told her I have to go home for Christmas, even though I'm planning the Canaries with Kelly and a few of the lads. I read about the case of Kitty Genovese in my basic psychology. She was a nurse in New York who was attacked in the street one night and killed. Lots of people were watching from their windows, and no one did anything, as everyone assumed someone else had called the police. They call it 'the bystander effect': too many people looking on and no one taking responsibility. That's what's happening with Sexy Sue.

## December 18th

I have a kind of meeting in the res with Kelly and Margaret and a few of the senior nurses. I start telling them about Kitty Genovese, and they look at me blankly. Then I say we have to do something about

Sexy Sue, as it seems like she hasn't left Fort Apache for a month or changed her clothes. But Christmas is coming, and we're all running out of steam.

## December 27th

I decided to call the cool-dude psychiatrist down to A&E today. Enough is enough – Sexy Sue was starting to smell almost as bad as the surgical Registrar, and that's saying something. I start rattling on about how worried we all are. He looks at me calmly and compassionately as I talk. Then he smiles and says he'll sort things out. A few hours later, they come for her.

## December 29th

Sexy Sue looked confused but relieved when she was being led out of Fort Apache up to the psychiatric unit. Margaret came over, called me a hero, then kissed me in front of the whole place. All the nurses started cheering. Poor Margaret – she's going to have a bad January. Later on, we all talk in the res. I tell them again about Kitty Genovese and the bystander effect, and now it all makes sense to them. Of course, I don't tell them the whole story about Sexy Sue. Back in September, I was outside a cubicle and overheard Sexy Sue talking to an elderly patient with heart failure. What she said had shocked me, but I'd decided not to do anything about it because I thought it might cause trouble. She had made the comment quietly, and for a while, I thought that maybe I had misheard her. But I'm pretty sure now that she definitely said it: "The reason you're sick is because you're evil."

# THE BLUE TROLL OF WINTER

Kevin Lally

There once lived a husband and wife with their dutiful young boy called Johan in a wooden cabin up north. During the summer, the skies are blue, the weather warm, and the living easy. But the winters are cold and dark and full of snow. As the coldest, snowiest days of winter approached, Johan and his father were out in the woods. His father swung his axe and told him not to wander too far, else the Blue Troll of Winter would steal him away and eat him. The boy didn't think the Blue Troll really existed. Nevertheless, he stayed within sight of his father and wore a bright red woollen coat, so he stood out against the trees. Johan searched among the roots and leaves for herbs, mushrooms and other helpful ingredients for his mother's healing recipes, for she was a keen herbalist.

Johan and his father took the dog sleigh to the village before the snow made it too difficult to cross the mountain pass. Johan brought some letters from his mother to the wise women – news and gossip, recipes, and patterns for knitting. In turn, the wise women gave Johan herbs and replies to his mother, as well as a small package as a gift. Johan's mother was much loved by the wise women; they had lived together like sisters before Johan's father came along.

The next day, his father decided to chop down a spruce tree and bring it into the cabin. He wanted to adorn it with red berries and candles to see his wife smile during the harsh season. With one swift sweep of the axe, he felled the young tree but then clutched at his heart and died.

The widow grieved earnestly for her husband, for he was a good man. He had built their cabin and always kept their bellies full by hunting reindeer for meat. She was also with child and worried how she would cope with young Johan and their cabin in the forest.

But Johan was brave and true. He gathered firewood, fed the dogs, and milked the Finncattle. When his mother couldn't sleep at night – when she wailed and screamed for her dead husband – he would stew valerian root in milk to help her rest. When his mother was tired and agitated and cursed everyone around her, he realised she had been eating juniper berries and crushed them under his foot. They were poisonous to unborn babies.

This latter encounter puzzled Johan, for it was his mother who had taught him herblore and the dangers of juniper berries. He wondered what she had been thinking and hoped she hadn't been thinking at all – the alternative was too terrible to bear. When the time came for the baby to arrive – when the snow was thickest and the days shortest – he was unsure what to do.

His mother forbade him from going to the village to get the wise women. Beads of sweat gathered on her forehead as she spat and told him they took glee in seeing her suffer and would try to steal the baby. They had always resented her for leaving them and having a husband, she cried, clutching her belly in pain.

Johan, knowing better than to talk back to his mother at this moment in time, boiled a pot of hot water and fetched a linen towel. He didn't think it was the job of seven-year-old boys to help birth children, but he hoped it wasn't much different to cattle.

His mother paced and refused to lie in bed. Her hair, usually long and chestnut-brown, seemed greyer now and was knotted like a sparrow's nest. When Johan tried to comb it out, she took the hairbrush from him and chased him around the room, threatening to beat him for making his father cut down that tree.

Despite his mother's confusion and Johan's uncertainties, the baby came without issue. Johan's new sister was called Ingeborg. Johan prepared porridge, honey and nuts for his mother, and she fed the baby.

The next day, his mother asked him to go and collect seven reindeer antlers for a remedy. It was not unusual for Johan to go out to collect ingredients for his mother – he had done it many times before. But he did not understand the pressing need so soon after his sister's birth. Nevertheless, he put on his favourite red woollen coat, gathered the dogs and took off on the sleigh.

While he was away, the mother told the baby, "Your evil brother will surely die by the Blue Troll's hands out in the snow tonight. His just rewards for killing your father."

It took Johan many hours to find seven reindeer antlers in the snow. Even with the dogs for protection, he worried about wolves or – and hated to admit this to himself – even the Blue Troll attacking. When he returned, he was very tired, but he gave his mother the antlers and prepared the dinner and cleaned the linen. He hoped the antlers were part of some new recipe the wise women had sent for helping to clear the mind after grief. That night, he slept a deep, dreamless sleep.

The next day, Johan's mother told him to go and collect seven large pine cones for a poultice. Johan had never heard of such a recipe, but he trusted she had some reason for such a strange request. When he went outside, he found the gate open – though he was sure he had secured it the night before – and all the dogs were gone. He was distraught, but he went and found his father's snowshoes and readied himself to find the pine cones.

His mother watched him leave through the window and said to her young babe, "Surely the Blue Troll will get your brother today. I chased his dogs away so he can only move slowly through the snow."

It took Johan even longer to find seven large pine cones on foot, but he finally succeeded and was happy. His mother threw them in the fire when he handed them to her, snow from outside still melting on his coat, and cursed him. Johan's father had taught him to respect his mother and do as he was told, so he did his chores and made the meals and fed himself and went to bed.

The next day, his mother told him he must go out and trap seven white hares and bring back their pelts, for she needed them to line the baby's crib. Johan couldn't find the snowshoes that he had left inside the door of the cabin, but he wrapped himself in his red woollen coat and set out early to set his traps anyway.

His mother cackled to herself and whispered to her sleeping daughter, "Surely the Blue Troll of Winter will find him and eat his bones now."

Johan had trapped hares with his father before, and he knew where the best places to set the traps were. But it was very slow-going, and by nightfall, he was far from home with only three hare pelts. As he struggled through the deep snow, he heard wolves howling and knew that a pack had caught his scent.

He made to run, but the faster he tried to move, the deeper he sunk into the powdery snow.

He came across a spruce tree with low branches. He stuffed the hare pelts into his coat and climbed the tree, hoping he could wait out the wolves overnight. Johan took one branch at a time, struggling to grip with his soggy mittens. The howls of the wolves drew closer, and Johan climbed faster. The branches were slippery, and his mittens were no help, so he shook them off and flung them into the bushes. A wolf emerged and pounced. Johan could see the moonlight in his eyes and screamed, pulling himself out of reach just in time. More pairs of eyes glinted in the darkness, each fighting for a share of the mittens. Johan sped up, reaching for the safer branches above. The hare pelts slipped out and tumbled down the tree to the ground. The wolves flung themselves at them. They snapped and snarled, shredding the hares to pieces in seconds. They looked up and saw Johan shaking on his branch. They hurled their bodies against the side of the tree in an effort to knock him down. Fingers numb with cold, Johan used the twine for the traps to lash himself to the tree in case he lost his grip.

The wolves showed no sign of losing interest until suddenly the sound of bells rang through the woods. At this, the wolves began to whimper and their tails tucked between their legs.

"The Blue Troll," Johan thought. His stomach

turned, and his breath quickened.

He could see less and less in the encroaching darkness, but the clanging of bells and the hiss of a sleigh skimming over snow was clear. When the sounds were closer, Johan could just about see a sleigh being drawn by seven reindeer crashing through the undergrowth. On it was the Blue Troll, thrashing a whip and yelling. The wolves scattered.

Johan heard the Troll shout, "Johan, come down from the tree! I will bring you home on my sleigh."

Johan didn't move. His whole life, he had been taught to fear the Blue Troll. The idea of putting his life in the troll's hands was not an attractive one. That said, he was certain that if he stayed in this tree, he would die in the freezing cold before morning. Reluctantly, Johan unfastened himself from the trunk, slid down the tree and approached the sleigh.

The Blue Troll was big – bigger than his father. He was dressed all in blue and had a thick white beard like the old men in the village. But he looked both older but fitter and stronger than those men.

"Are you the Blue Troll of Winter?" asked Johan, who was bold now in the face of certain death.

"Ho, ho, ho! Some do call me that, but the magic that exists in these bones is not Trollish. You can call me *Joulupukki*," he said. Before Johan could ask any more questions (for his mind was full of whys and wherefores), they were away, racing through the snow faster than Johan thought possible. They pulled up at a cut spruce tree, and under the light of Joulupukki's torches, Johan saw this was the spot where his father had died.

Joulupukki heaved the tree onto the back of his sleigh and took a spruce cone from his pocket. He planted it in the ground and said, "Ho, ho, ho! Here will be a fine tree to remember your father by." With a crack of his whip, they were off once more.

Joulupukki was able to find Johan's cabin without any direction. But when Johan tried to open the door, he found it was locked.

"Ho, ho, ho! No problem for me," said Joulupukki, and he jumped up onto the roof and dived down the chimney. He opened the door to Johan and gathered the tree from the sleigh.

Inside, they found Johan's mother talking – whether to herself or to the baby, it was not clear. She seemed shocked and annoyed to see Joulupukki, but when she saw Johan, she burst into a fit of rage. "You did it. You did this. You killed my husband and cursed my baby! And now you bring this Troll here to kill me!"

Johan was shocked into silence. But Joulupukki just smiled and said, "Ho, ho, ho. There is darkness here as black as night," and took Johan's mother by the temples. Blue sparks fizzled from his fingertips, and Johan's mother jumped and moved as if she was having a fit. The huge Joulupukki placed her gently onto the bed and watched for a few moments as the fit took over. He turned to Johan and flashed him a warm, reassuring smile. "Ho, ho, ho, don't fret, young Johan. When she awakes in the morrow, the darkness will have left her."

With a flourish, he flung the spruce tree into the corner of the room, and from his pockets he slung pinecones and acorns, nuts and berries, ribbons and bright fabrics across the tree, decorating it just how Johan's father had described. From his other pocket, he fished a small wooden sleigh and gave it to Johan. "Ho, ho, ho, a gift for you, dear boy!" Then he took a wooden doll from his other pocket and tucked it into the little girl's blankets. "Ho, ho, ho, a gift for Ingeborg, too." With that, he left out the front door as easily as he entered through the chimney, jumped back onto the sleigh and took the reins. With a smile and wink, he waved, and the sleigh started to move.

Johan chased after him and shouted, "Joulupukki, Joulupukki, wait, wait. I have a gift for you!" As he ran, Johan shrugged himself free of his favourite red woollen coat, his finest possession. He offered it to Joulupukki, his breath clouding in the iced air.

Joulupukki's eyes widened in surprise at the kind gesture and said, "Ho, ho, ho! Johan, I could never take your red woollen coat. But look, I shall remember thee!" With a flourish, his blue suit turned the reddest red. "Ho, ho, ho! They won't call me the Blue Troll of Winter anymore!" And off he went, never to be seen by Johan again.

The next day, Johan's mother woke up and greeted Johan as if she hadn't seen him for a year. She hugged him and loved him again and forever more.

# BOB MOONEY

## Henry O'Connell

So, this is the famous Dalkey. It feels a bit different from home, all right. There's a certain feeling in the air. It's a mixture of things, I suppose: there's the sea nearby and the slightly better weather, it being on the east coast. It's warmer too, with more sunshine and less wind and rain…but there's something else too. The air feels rarefied. *That's* the feeling: rarefied air.

I'm sure all the money around this place has an effect on the air, too. Or maybe it's the rarefied air that attracts the people with money. It feels like this place has been wealthy for hundreds of years; layers of wealth upon wealth, from the Victorian Harbour at Dun Laoghaire in the north, to Coliemore Harbour, Dalkey Island and Killiney Bay in the south. They say that there are seven castles in the Dalkey area alone. That's a lot of history and wealth accumulated in one place. And Dalkey Island was used as a trading post by the Vikings before Dublin itself ever became a port of importance. The Vikings ran a slave trade, and they would kidnap Irish women, barter for them on Dalkey Island and then take them off on one-way voyages to places like Iceland. They say that practically all Icelandic women can trace their genes back to Ireland. Those poor kidnapped women became the unwilling mothers of a whole nation.

So, the people around Dalkey have been used to trading and making money for hundreds, maybe even thousands, of years. And they're used to stealing women. The people here look better-dressed, shinier, more tanned, and more manicured than the people in the west. They drive big SUVs and sports cars through the narrow streets and leafy driveways. They walk upright. They exude confidence. They seem like they don't notice me, like I'm another species, or maybe even invisible. And when they talk to each other, you can hear exactly what they're saying from yards away. They enunciate everything clearly, with confidence and emphasis, like everything they say is important and should be heard. Americans are a bit like that, too. Maybe that's the way you get when you live in a place like this, or again maybe it's places like this that attract people like that.

The people out west, where I come from, are shy and meek. They whisper their words and mutter under their breaths as if they're afraid they might be overheard. Maybe it's because of generations of being an oppressed people. Maybe that's why we whisper and nod and wink. During the War of Independence a hundred years ago, the British soldiers and police used to swagger around our village with their pistols held out to frighten and suppress my grandfather's generation. They would fire off into the sky hundreds of rounds on machine guns that they had brought back with them from places like the Somme. They would spend hours firing into the night sky while the people in the village and countryside around lay in their beds awake, frozen stiff with fear and humiliation.

I'm sitting here in Dalkey, parked up in my dirty old banger of a car, waiting patiently outside Bob Mooney's house. He is very much like the rest of them here: attractive, wealthy, effortlessly confident, one of life's winners. I haven't met him yet, but I know him very well from his radio show and his relationship with my wife. I need to meet him, because he has ruined my marriage and my life. You see – and this is a hard thing to say – but my wife has been in love with him for over twenty years. I'm not sure how much contact they've had, but it's been enough to break us apart. He is a filthy Viking who has taken my wife from me. Though unfortunately, unlike the enslaved Irish women of a thousand years ago, I believe that my wife has been his willing captive.

I can remember when the problem started. We had been married a few years and were hoping to have children, but nothing was happening. We had all the tests and scans done, and each one came back clear. The official diagnosis was that nothing was wrong.

We just needed to be patient – as if patience running out wasn't the reason we'd had all the tests in the first place. Sheila was starting to get older, and she was anxious to get pregnant as soon as possible. We tried very hard, to a point where we started to get tired of sleeping with each other, and I moved into the spare room – we both needed a break from the whole thing. It didn't help that we were under pressure with regard to money: I only had a small job in the cardboard box factory and a few sheep. In the evenings, I dabbled in my pointless painting and poetry.

It was around that time that I noticed how often she mentioned Bob Mooney in our conversations. She would listen to his radio show while she was at home during the day and then quote his advice and supposed wisdom to me in the evening. "Bob Mooney has saved us a fortune in grocery bills with his advice," she might say. Or she might correct something I had said by quoting Bob Mooney. I told her I thought we should treat ourselves and buy a new microwave, and she would say something like, "Well, Bob doesn't think they're good for you."

At first, I didn't take much notice of these comments, but then they started to get under my skin. It wasn't just his advice on household matters. She seemed to have gotten to know the essence of his personality.

"Oh, poor Bob was so upset last week after that journalist died – she was his friend, you know. I felt so sorry for him. I thought he was going to cry, but of course, he'd never do that."

Nothing *I* said ever seemed to interest her, but everything *he* said seemed to be a source of endless fascination. The odd time I got home early from the factory, I would watch her listening to her dear Bob. She would glide around the kitchen in a mesmerised state and shush me if I said anything, making me wait until the ad breaks before she would even look at me.

This fascination of hers was starting to get to me even more when she suddenly became pregnant. We had only slept together the odd time in the past few months, far less than before, so I was surprised. She told me she had been watching her cycles, and she had timed our last night together for when she was ovulating. We were both happy and relieved when the pregnancy test showed that little blue line of positivity – it had been a long wait. But it all seemed a bit...*odd* to me. I wasn't completely happy, for some reason that I couldn't figure out.

We were talking in the kitchen one evening when she was around six months gone.

"It really feels like a miracle baby after all our waiting," she said. As she said it, she looked at the radio, which was turned off at the time. And in the space of a second or two, I suddenly realised what was going on. I felt hot and shivery. I thought my head would explode. Mooney had impregnated her through the radio waves.

Doctors would later look at me with a quizzical look when I told them about that day, but I knew the truth. During the subsequent years of hell, each time I met a new junior doctor in the psychiatric clinic, I would tell them the story. It was the same every time: they would listen intently until I got to the part about Sheila getting pregnant through the radio waves. Then the shutters would come down over their eyes, and you would see a subtle sign of relief on the doctor's face that said, "Ah yes, he's clearly unwell. He needs to stay on those medications. I'll see him again in three months."

When the baby finally came, I would have nothing to do with him. It made me sick to look at him. She called him Michael, after her father. In my mind, I called him Bob Junior. She asked me numerous times why I wouldn't hold him or help her with him. I tried to explain that I was tired and stressed from work and not having enough money to support them, but I don't think she believed me. I always avoided being left alone with him. He was Bob Mooney's son, so I didn't *want* to be alone with him. I went from having no feelings for the boy to outright hatred towards him over the next few years. And I couldn't be alone with him in case I acted on my hatred for him and his father and harmed him in some way or even killed him. Mooney had done enough to me. I wasn't going to spend the rest of my life in jail while he sat in a studio up in Dublin, charming my wife through the radio waves every day. A few people in the town knew, too. I could see it in them. She and Mooney had made a show of me.

Bob Junior got bigger, and I hated him more and more each day. He learned not to talk to me or come to me for anything – at least he had that good sense. Sheila grew tired of my ways. She thought I was lazy and neglectful of the two of them. But the truth was that I couldn't stomach being with them. She had betrayed me, and she was continuing to betray me. Harming the boy could have been Bob Mooney's jail bait for me; I wouldn't fall into his trap.

After a few years simmering away like this, it all came out one sunny Saturday afternoon in June when the boy was around four. I came home early to find Sheila and him dancing around the kitchen to some tune on the radio. I stood at the kitchen door watching them, envious of how effortlessly happy they were. So, this was what they were like when they thought I couldn't see them.

When the music stopped, it was Mooney's voice that came on: "I really hope you both enjoyed that, my darling Sheila and Bob Junior."

I rushed across the kitchen floor and grabbed the two of them. "Out!" I shouted at them as I pushed them along the hallway and out the front door. I remember the look of terror in the boy's eyes, so awful he almost made me stop in my tracks. But I wouldn't fall for it. His father had taught him that look. He thought he could soften me up with that look. But I had had enough of the two of them. Mooney the Viking raider had stolen my wife and impregnated her. He was starting a nation of descendants, and this nasty boy was the first of them. Their presence in my house was a source of disgust and humiliation to me. Their chat and laughter were like the sound of the British gunfire used to terrorise my grandparents.

After that day, there were months of Gardaí interviews and meetings with solicitors and social workers. There were psychiatric assessments. In the end, it was me who got kicked out of my own house. I had to move into a little flat in the town, and she stayed on with Bob Junior in our house, *my* house. The psychiatrists told me that I had an unusual version of 'morbid jealousy' and prescribed me antipsychotic medication. They tried to get me into the hospital a few times, but I was always well able to talk my way out of their traps and tricks.

"These medications may help. But geographical separation is really the only way to deal with a situation like this," one of them told me, as if he was reading instructions from a manual on psychiatric disorders. Of course, it made no sense to me.

Now the boy is seven. I have not seen him or Sheila for three full years, but I think of nothing else except the two of them. At first, I kept a few of my sheep, but I lost the job in the factory because I had a lot of arguments with the lads there. Then the sheep were taken from me. I told the farm inspector that some of the sheep were sleeping in the field, but he kept saying that they were dead. There was no talking to him. Imagine my shame: a farmer having his animals taken from him. They came for them in a big truck one morning and, as the truck drove away with them, I realised that I had reached the end. Maybe Mooney had something to do with the sheep, too. I wouldn't tell anyone about that. As soon as I mentioned Mooney's name to anyone, they switched off, as they assumed it was clear evidence that I was crazy.

So here I am in my dirty clothes, sitting in my old car on the side of the road near where I think Bob Mooney lives. Sheila is gone from me. Mooney's son is living with her in my house. I'm sure that the three of them get together every day through the radio and have a good laugh about me. They really did a number on me.

I tried reasoning with Sheila a few years back, but she would have none of it. As soon as I mentioned Bob Mooney, she would roll her eyes and fold her arms. I have never spoken to the boy, and I never will now.

I've researched Mooney's background and made a few subtle enquiries, and I think I'm close to his house. There's a high wall in front, with electric gates. I've been sitting here in my car for two days and two nights, waiting for the gates to open and for him to go in or come out. And I have rehearsed everything down to the last syllable and move. When I see him drive in or out, I will start my car and ram into the side of his. Then I will take the shotgun from under my seat and blow his brains out. I will have a few minutes to get to Killiney Hill, where I'll dump the car in the car park and run with the second loaded shotgun up to the Obelisk. From there I will ring Sheila. Even if she doesn't answer, I will leave a message telling her that I have slain her lover and won the long war. Then I will stick the shotgun in my mouth and leave this world on my terms, victorious at last.

# THE WALL

Frank McKenna

He left the hospital, minutes after nine. The low morning sun stung his eyes and burned his forehead as he walked to his recently acquired Mondeo. He knew Dee would be up by now, checking her watch until he arrived. He just didn't know how much of him would get there. How much of him remained.

He turned the key and set off.

Somehow, last night had been the most depleting night he could remember. It remained draped over him even as he put more distance between himself and the hospital, like a predator weighing down exhausted prey, its teeth already sunk into his neck. Patient after patient. Crisis after crisis. Many details had faded, blended into the mix.

He couldn't remember the name of that blogger who kept saying she didn't trust herself. Over and over again. Slipping it in after describing arguments with her boyfriend or the infuriating jealousy of her friends. Flicking her eyes to his to see if he'd bit on it. He might look her up once he arrived. See if she'd posted about the crisis in her *mental health*. He half suspected she might have recorded the whole thing. At least she was now home in the care of her loving and tormented family.

And there was that Jamie-Something, who pushed the ED nurse. Security didn't like that. A six-foot, ripped nineteen-year-old standing bare-chested in the aisle between X-Ray and CDU, off his head, shouting and spraying spittle, while terrified, deathly sick pensioners cowered on their trolleys. That's what happens when you spend four days in your bedroom taking a lucky dip of party pills you bought on the internet.

It was actually called a *Lucky Dip Bag*. That's what he ordered. For eighty euros on his mother's credit card. And it set his mind on fire. It was quite something to be alone with someone that wound up, to sit calmly while the frothing beast prowled the room, and to talk it down.

But Alice Regan, she was different.

After an hour of driving, he turned onto the top of the main street in Kilkee. He lowered the window out of habit. He let the salty air seep in and through him.

Even this early, footpaths were busy with summer-clad amblers and buggy-pushers and dog walkers brushing past inflatable dolphins and boogie boards. Yellow and red and blue windmills whirled in stands outside shops, and stands of postcards shivered in the breeze. Tourists were sipping coffee, carrying French sticks and ice cream and bags of bonbons. Heading up or heading down, bumping into acquaintances. Everyone knew someone here. Half of Limerick came to Kilkee on long weekends. All in glorious, easygoing colour.

But today, there was not the usual easing of tension in his shoulders. His nose was not tickled by seaweed and periwinkles. And he glided slowly through the light, slow traffic, not registering the figures or faces.

At the bottom of the main street, he turned right, driving slowly along the coastline of the horseshoe bay. He stopped as children crossed to the beach in a convoy of primary-coloured buckets and spades.

Past the beach, the bay sank further from the road. The waist-high wall that ran along the footpath became a jagged, rocky cliff on the other side. There was a particular point on the wall from where a solid jump would clear the cliff face and allow the daring to plummet fifty feet into the Atlantic. This was known by those who spent their childhood summers in Kilkee as *The Wall*. He had stood atop it twice in his life, on his seventeenth and eighteenth summers, and twice he had stepped back down into the group of his taunting friends, shaking and embarrassed. Passing it still sent a sharp needle of dissatisfaction through him.

Around the next corner, he turned through the

stone gate of their apartment block. Dee was sitting on a deck chair on the first-floor balcony, perched over the car park, square-on to the midday sun. Her long, slim legs were crossed, oversized sunglasses perched on a closed-mouth smile. She held up a glass of white wine.

As he got out of the car, she rose and leant on the balcony railing. "You look tired," she said.

"You look like a girl on holiday," he replied, reaching for his bags in the back seat.

He walked through the archway beneath her and climbed the stairs, short reels from the night before still playing; a subtle shift in Alice Regan's hard, young face, her ocean-green eyes picking at something in the back of his mind.

But Dee's wetsuit was drying on the railing outside the apartment door, and it got him wondering if she'd had an early dip this morning. This was something better to think about.

"Come on out," she called from the balcony. "I've poured you a glass."

The first day of their holidays had always meant sipping white wine through morning, soaking into the week ahead, sifting out what needed to be left behind. Dee would usually doze off around lunchtime while he people-watched from their perch.

"Have we got our timing wrong again?" he asked, emerging onto the balcony and leaning over to kiss her.

They both looked out at the ominous billow of

clouds approaching over the Atlantic, heralding the end of a five-day blue-sky spell.

"No pronouncements, please. I'm basking."

The wine was too dry. He sat, still in his work clothes: navy pants and a creased white shirt. It was the business-casual brown shoes that were most out of place, kicked up on the legs of the deck chair.

"How was it?"

"Exhausting," he said, lying back, feeling the warmth on his face and closing his eyes behind the Ray-Bans he had picked up last week. Alice Regan's eyes were right in front of him.

Dee tipped her glasses down to look at him.

"Leave it behind," she said. "You need this."

The next thing he was aware of was a shriek cutting through his slumber.

"Bobby!"

He looked down through the metal spokes of the balcony to see a woman racing into the middle of the road, buggy abandoned on the footpath. She was reaching out to grab a little boy – Bobby, he presumed – who was maybe two or three, red-faced, crying, mid-tantrum, and who had stopped traffic in both directions.

"The poor woman," said Dee, glancing up from the last few pages of her book. "Nice snooze? You missed all the sun."

He stretched in the chair, reaching his arms out to the sky.

The sun had indeed been chased away. The Atlantic had lost its shimmer. His glass of wine was still full on the table beside him, duller now than before.

He closed his eyes again, tempted back to the thickness of sleep.

"I said we'd meet Joe and Sandra at seven. Go for a bite. We could leave it for later in the week if you'd prefer?"

"No," he said. "We should go."

He sat up straight and planted his feet on the floor. Initially, there was just a sense of something hovering on the borders of consciousness, something he ought not to forget. Then she returned.

Alice Regan's was not an unusual presentation. A young woman in distress. A steady ramping up of inner tensions over weeks and months until, last night, the spilling over had led her to the Emergency Department.

Urgent assessments were not new to her, but she had not presented for over eighteen months – a long time in her world. And, unlike before, it was not that some argument or rejection had sent her spiralling into an acute, unboundaried dysphoria. No. This time it was regret. This time, the smouldering bridges in her past had all caught fire, and all she could see were the flames.

When he asked Alice if she had been thinking of ending her life, those eyes had locked with his. They assessed him. They appraised the situation. Slowly, they unlocked their hold, and slowly Alice shook her head.

She wanted to go home. She asserted that she had to go home. Hospital had not been good for her in the past, and he had agreed.

"These things," he had said. "These things you did and these things you didn't do – the more time that passes…."

Even after she had walked out of the emergency department doors, he continued to find himself locked in the grip of her eyes. He wondered now, hours later, what her thoughts had been in that moment. Did they contain a fragment of insight that the future could be different, or were they resigned and settled on a single course of action?

Dee began to read again, turning to the last page of her book.

"Are you enjoying it?" he asked.

"One sec," she said. "Nearly done."

It was difficult to imagine himself ever again being so caught up in the trivialities of a novel.

He looked at his phone, drawn to check for contact about last night's patients. The only reason for any such contact would be if something had gone horribly wrong. He wondered if the stakes in his world had become too high.

"You going to relax?" asked Dee, her book now closed on her lap.

He thought about telling her. Explaining how he could still feel himself in the presence of a young woman, that last night had been different from all the other nights. That he couldn't shake it off.

But it wasn't just Alice. On the drive down, he had counted eighteen people in crisis that he had seen that week. Five last night. Some asking for help, some being dragged to it. One taken by the Gardaí and all others sent home with a plan; most very grateful, two angry parents and one green-eyed Alice Regan. In too short a time, there had been too many. And too many of them young. All that risk had been accumulating inside him, decision after decision: admit to the hospital or send home with a plan. It raced around his head, unnamed and undefined. It restricted his breath.

He knew that no matter how many good decisions he made in the dead of night, if he saw enough people, something was eventually going to go wrong. He had been told this by every consultant psychiatrist who had ever tried to teach him anything, and he could feel it in every interaction with a patient. He couldn't read minds, and he couldn't account for something changing after they walked out the door. One bit of bad news, one impulsive thought shot out of the proverbial blue, and that could be it.

He stood and leant on the railing and looked out over the bay. As an infant, he had been plonked on that sand, and it had wreaked havoc in the creases of his skin. He'd been carried to the water and tossed in the air and had his toes dipped in the stinging, cold Atlantic.

He was nine when he first leapt from the pier. He had felt such a thrill as his back foot left the concrete and he soared over the ocean – for a few seconds, he had been *flying*. No moment in his life had caused such an explosion of adrenaline inside him like that time in the air. When he resurfaced, he was invincible. He was all-conquering.

Until years later, when he faced The Wall and his invincibility abruptly dissolved, replaced by a pounding in his chest and a tremor in his legs, when he learnt how a single moment could live inside him, could infiltrate him and taint him – something unconquered, forgotten by everyone other than himself.

"I might just go for a swim," he said.

"Really? It's probably going to rain."

He looked up at the clouds again, at the darkened sky.

"You want me to come?" she asked.

"No," he said. "I just need to wash everything off. Dip in and out."

He left her with her hands resting on her book, her eyelids heavy.

Wearing only his swimming togs and grasping a rolled-up towel in his hand, he followed the footpath, heading east along the strand. As he rounded the bend out of sight of their balcony, the sky succumbed to the inevitable, and the first drops fell, cold on his bare shoulders.

On the beach, bags were being packed, and chairs and windbreakers folded up. People moved faster on the footpath, breaking into jogs behind their buggies, yanking their dogs along by the leads.

Today, Alice Regan would receive a phone call from a nurse. Most likely, that would go well – things would be *held* – and she would be seen in the Day Hospital on Monday. Most likely. The odds were overwhelmingly in his, and Alice's, favour. She would be fine.

But there was always that minuscule chance.

The rain had become heavy. He passed through a gap in the stone wall and stood at the top of the steps that led down to the diving boards – the high board and the low board. The tide was in. He could have a couple of dives, immerse in the cold saltwater and go home. That might do it.

But he didn't step down.

Instead, he back-tracked to the point where the grass verge and the cliff-face jutted out the least. The point deemed the only safe place to drop from that crazy height. The pinnacle of Kilkee's jumping challenges. The Wall.

Streams now ran down his forehead into his eyes, down his cheeks, down his back and front, until they dripped from the hem of his shorts. The raindrops hammered the path and the wall and the grass. He lay his soaking towel down. In a moment, he had pushed himself up and onto The Wall, standing atop it.

He tilted into the rain, and a tremble shook his legs.

Over the bay, the line of the horizon had blurred into a strip – a vague evolution in the texture of darkness. To his right, the town was being washed clean.

The fear was familiar. The pounding in his chest. The quickened breathing. A boy's terror.

But now there were thoughts too, when before there had been nothing but a raging wildfire. Alice was there. Her eyes and her tears and all of her regret mingled with his own and filled him.

He raised his arms to the sides and turned his palms into the onslaught.

He thought of Dee, who would by now have taken indoors and be marvelling at the beauty of the rain. Who would light up when he returned home, dripping.

When he jumped, his chest roared. It surged from his core and burst through his toes and fingertips. It lengthened the milliseconds, making it seem as though the fall was lasting longer than it should.

When he hit the water, he sank and sank as the sea gulped and closed above him.

The descent slowed and eventually stopped and, after a split-second pause, he began to kick. He arrowed to what he thought was upwards, but for a few desperate moments, he wasn't sure. Then the ceiling became brighter, and brighter, and patterned by a nail-bed of impacting raindrops. He broke the surface face-first, vacuuming what he could: air, rain, life.

He continued to kick his legs slowly and began to wave ellipses with his hands. After a minute or so, he front-crawled toward the diving boards, every stroke bringing him closer until a swell hoisted him to where he could clutch the metal ladder bolted to the cliff face. He climbed the few rungs to the plateau by the lower board, where he first learned to dive as a child, and found his footing. He roared a cry into the air of everything inside him, and no one could hear it but the sea and the sky and the rocks and the rain.

# TIREDNESS KILLS

Kevin Lally

My name is Doctor Anthony Clooney, and I currently reside in the Central Mental Hospital. Working as a consultant psychiatrist for ten years, I have never been successful in referring dangerous and psychotic patients to the CMH. You basically have to kill someone to get in. So how does a consultant psychiatrist find *himself* admitted to Ireland's highest security Forensic Prison? Well, it all starts with a rugby match....

## Thomond Park, Limerick, 2002

I pull on the jersey – the sky blue of St Xavier's College – and gather around the coach, jostling shoulder-to-shoulder with my teammates. A challenge match: Leinster School's champions versus Munster's. There is no trophy on the line, just pride, glory and the privilege of wearing the school jersey one last time. The team talk ends, and we recite the school motto:

## *Ad Majorem Dei Gloriam*
### (To the Greater Glory of God)

We half-march, half-jog onto the field, and the noise of the crowd engulfs us—parents, teachers, friends, all cheering.

Our kick-off; we go long to put their rookie winger under pressure. I chase him down, ready to make an early big tackle, to set a precedent. I make eye contact, dive and…nothing. A sneaky sidestep and he is gone up the wing and I'm on my arse. A sign of things to come.

With five minutes to go, I'm battered and bruised but probably faring the best out of the team. We are four points up, score 9-5, three penalties. All gifted from poor discipline from the Munchin's forwards. Not afraid to throw a dig.

Their scrum in the centre of the pitch at the halfway line, and I see a backline move emerging a mile off.

"Heads up, boys, they're splitting their backs."

The scrum goes their way, and I see they're going to my side. Eight makes a half-hearted break, but I don't commit. He draws in our nine and pops to his scrum-half. I don't have him: he's just out of reach, but I know where he's going. A wide pass to the rookie winger. I line him up for a smash. He sees me coming, a cheeky wink. I'd like to say it was a stiff hand-off, but it was more like a dismissive slap. I can't get near him – he swats me off then pirouettes. He's gone.

Our fullback won the national 110m hurdles. He'll catch him, tap tackle. So, I get up and chase, to compete at the breakdown. The Munchin's winger is faster, though, and it's not close. He runs in under the posts, unopposed. 10-9. The conversation is made, and it's 12-9. Game over.

People start chanting his name, "Cooney! Cooney! Cooney!"

Only a month ago, it was *my* name chanted from the stands of Lansdowne Road, the best rugby stadium in Ireland; it sounds eerily similar, which exacerbates the humiliation. Afterwards, there's tea and sandwiches and a few pints in the club bar before we get back on the coach to Dublin. I do my sound guy routine and go over to the rookie winger.

"Good game today, kid." I offer my hand.

"Yeah, thanks." He takes my hand in his and shakes, and for a moment, it's like I'm trapped in a sinewy vice grip.

"Leinster School's champions?" he says.

"Yeah, we beat Black—"

"So what?" he interrupts. "Good luck in the Leavin'." He sneers and turns his back to me. The Irish Leaving Certificate, a set of exams that will define what we'll do for the next few years and probably the rest of our lives.

It's 4th May, only a month until that big quiz starts. Even if I started studying now, I'd never get into a good course. The rugby dream is over, so I have to start a new one. I open the CAO handbook, the big list of courses and the required entry grades: Medicine, 560 points. So, it's Grind school for me. 9 a.m. to 5 p.m. classes and 5 p.m. to 10 p.m. supervised study, five grand a year. Better than going to a local tech and doing agricultural science, though.

## M7, Co Tipperary, 2020

We're cruising down the M7, doing a very safe 110 kilometres per hour. Our Volvo XC90 was voted Ireland's safest and most reliable family car. Looks ugly, but we don't mind. We're on our way back from IKEA, and the boot is full of furniture for the nursery. A little impromptu journey, and at first, I wasn't on board. At thirty-nine weeks, it was a bit dodgy. I didn't want her to deliver our kid on a sofa in IKEA. However, I've done my homework over the last few months and reckon I could do a C-section if I was forced.

You have to pick your battles with a pregnant partner.

"Claude if a boy, Cleo if a girl," Leah says. We've done the scans, but we elected not to know the sex.

"Claude Clooney, Cleo Clooney," I repeat out loud, letting their full names roll over my tongue. She likes a bit of alliteration. Not bad.

"How about Luke Clooney?" I try to say it nonchalantly.

"Luke. Luke? That better not be someone from

*Star Trek.*" Leah grins. She likes to pretend she doesn't know the difference between *Star Wars* and *Star Trek*.

One car, two people, three heartbeats. I see a road sign up ahead that reads:

## Maraíonn Tuirse
## TIREDNESS KILLS

I like to remark to Leah that it's a grim name for a town. Leah still laughs, though we both know it's been a long time since that was funny.

She wants to pee and get a Burger King. I want to tell her we're only ten minutes away from the house in Castleconnell, but the little voice in my head says, *Pick your battles.* For the first time in our lives, we survived a trip to IKEA without a two-hour mutual sulk on the way home. I put this down to our morning session of transcendental meditation. During these sessions, I focus on the image of a blue lightsaber, and repeat my mantra. *Fear is the path to the dark side. Fear leads to anger. Anger leads to hate. Hate leads to suffering.* Copyright George Lucas. Thanks, George.

"Will you wear a mask?"

She sighs. I pull into the service station in Birdhill. It's got a shop, a Costa Coffee, a Burger King, and a sandwich bar. It takes Leah time to clamber out of the car, one leg at a time, back aching, wrists and ankles swollen. We wear masks. I like to tell her that we doctors and nurses are the prefects of

Irish society and must set a good example. I wonder if she is thinking, *Pick your battles*, too.

I queue for food. Leah nips off to the loo, where the line is long and slow-moving with all the social distancing. I'm back before her and have the seats. There is a large man across the way, with a mullet and a triple chin. Reminds me of Dr Sheehan, our consultant obstetrician. The man is stabbing his straw through the plastic opening in the cup, just like Sheehan did the procedure for genetic testing of the baby. Leah thought he was a pig; he reminded me more of Jabba the Hutt. He gave Leah a prescription for an anti-emetic tablet. His handwriting worse than mine, like a mixture of hieroglyphics and wingdings. But apparently, he was the best in the business. He could do a C-section in seven minutes.

Leah comes back from the bathroom and is oblivious to Jabba and the cup. She is about to sit down when a grey-haired woman approaches us. Her mask is only covering her mouth, and her nose peaks out like a beak.

"The size of you; must be twins."

There is an awkward silence. She probably means well. Leah attempts to be nice but I'm in before her....

"Mind your own business, big nose."

The old woman gasps and scuffles off like a horseshoe crab, a living fossil.

"You didn't need to be rude," Leah gently rebuffs.

"Fuck that; the time for politeness is long gone."

We drive through Castleconnell and down Bog Road. It's still bright, the start of May, the days getting that little bit longer. We drive by the houses with horses in their front gardens. I tell Leah a professional boxer used to live in one of these houses. I know she knows this, and she knows I know she knows, but I like to say it anyway.

We drive by the bigger houses with the stables for the horses. "The Prof lives in there," I tell her.

She nods, half asleep.

We arrive at our house, twice as big as what you'd get in Dublin for the same money. Big garden, big shed. I help Leah to bed first, and then I do my round. I check the emergency hospital bag: clothes, knickers, nursing bras, bottles, nappies, paracetamol in case they get stingy, phone charger (we've got the same brand of phone, so one will do), water and energy bars (the one Leah likes, but really, they're for me). I also pack a set of scrubs, a yellow hospital gown, gloves and masks. They have some restrictions on partners in the hospital during the COVID-19 pandemic, but I'll work around that.

I check the surgical scalpel in the front pocket of the bag. For an extreme emergency, if I have to do a Caesarean. I assisted on one fifteen years ago, but I've watched the YouTube videos since – easiest surgical procedure in the field of medicine.

It's 3am, and Leah gets up to go to the toilet. Nothing unusual about that. I check my phone. I've checked Google Maps for estimated journey times to the Maternity Hospital at different times of the day. Nineteen minutes door to door at 3am.

"Contractions have started," Leah says.

"You sure? Sure they're not—"

"Of course I'm sure," she snaps before I can get the words *Braxton Hicks* out of my mouth.

She *is* a trained midwife, I concede to myself.

"Better get going so." I have the hospital switchboard on speed-dial. "Hello, this is Dr Anthony Clooney. I will be arriving at the hospital in nineteen minutes with Leah Clooney. We are booked in under the care of Dr Sheehan...I know it's 3am; ring him and get him out of bed. I didn't spend five grand for him to get a good night's sleep."

We're in the car eventually and going across the city. No traffic, but it's dark and lashing rain. Classic Limerick weather: rain practically horizontal as the wind pushes it across. We pull up to the hospital; I remark on the sign that still reads *St Munchin's*, the old name for the maternity hospital. Reminds me of Kieran Cooney, the little bollox.

I'm wearing my blue hospital scrubs with *Maternity* written on them. They didn't fit ten years ago when I was a medical student here on my obstetrics rotation – much too baggy – but they fit now, with a bit of a squeeze. I also have my swipe, which, two months ago, I got authorised for activating the doors in the maternity hospital on the grounds of being a liaison psychiatrist. I've stuffed my old stethoscope into my pocket – haven't worn that for years, but it might come in handy later. I also have an admission booklet, which I've taken the effort to fill out myself to ensure all the details are correct concerning Leah's medical and obstetric history.

I'm into reception in a flash and back out with a wheelchair. I get the umbrella from the boot, press the button, and it automatically extends, the blue canopy opening with a swish like a lightsaber.

I shield Leah from the rain as we move from the car into the building. She's doing the breathing, and I murmur all those things people are supposed to say, "You're doing great, deep breaths now."

I take the right turn for the elevator; the labour ward is on the second floor.

"Excuse me. Excuse me! Where are you going?" a receptionist or a midwife bleats from somewhere behind me.

"We're going to the labour ward. Where else do you think we're going?"

"You can't just do that; you have to be checked in."

"I rang twenty minutes ago. Leah Clooney, get the chart from records. I have the admission booklet here. Bleep the junior doctor and get Sheehan in here, now!"

I don't wait for either the confirmation or the denial. My swipe activates the staff lift, which is closer, and up we go. In the care plan, we've gone for a "home birth". Initially, Leah wanted to use a doula, which is like the obstetric equivalent of homoeopathy. We compromised by opting for the home delivery suite, which is also on the second floor. It's basically a hospital room done up in the style of a 1980s' kitchen, but with a giant bath in the middle.

We approach the midwife's station; I crouch so they can't see me but keep pushing Leah's wheelchair along. Leah just waves at the midwives as we go by. I keep going until I find the Home Delivery Suite. There isn't much monitoring equipment inside, just the CTG machine – the one with the graph paper, used to measure the foetal heartbeat.

Eventually, we are assigned a midwife, and everyone is cross with me. There is some suggestion I shouldn't be here, that I shouldn't have barged in. I call their bluff on calling the Gardaí, and here we are. The midwife dressed in pink scrubs is filling out her notes, and I continue with the birth plan by setting up the speakers for the music and getting the scented candles out.

One of the junior doctors comes in. She has clearly been briefed. "Hi, my name is Dr Louise O'Donnell. I'm the doctor on call. How's Leah doing?" She directs her attention to Leah and pretends I'm not there.

I let them get on with it. She wants to check my admission booklet, which is fair enough. Gives me enough time to look her up on the Medical Council website. Graduated from Galway in 2018. One year of intern training, and this is her first obstetrics job.

"Just a moment, please, Dr O'Donnell. Have you alerted Dr Sheehan that one of his private patients has been admitted to the labour ward?"

"No. Dr Sheehan isn't actually on-call tonight." Her words rise like a red lightsaber.

"But this is his *private* patient. We had his word he would attend." I click on my lightsaber. The blue light emerges from the handle, ionising the air, a brief crackle.

"The labour is progressing quite slowly and safely based on the CTG and the contractions." The red lightsaber swings.

"But have you contacted the consultant on-call to inform them of the risks and ask for advice?" I block.

"What risk factors?" Blue slices past red. A minor flesh wound.

"Maternal age, prima gravida and pre-term delivery. I think this is slightly above the pay scale of a first-year doctor. Can you make an entry in the notes stating that the patient's advocate made a request for the responsible treating consultant and the consultant on-call to be contacted and your rationale for refusing to do the same?" Blue swings through the air and swipes – a decapitation.

She leaves the room.

I remember my own training, difficult people questioning rank and experience. They were usually pompous, arrogant, dysfunctional families looking for somewhere to displace their anxiety, or – when things went wrong – their blame. But on the other side of the curtain, the quality of junior doctors and even senior doctors is like playing roulette. You spin a wheel and hope you get someone who is not just kind and compassionate, but *competent*. The other thing I learned is that the patients that kick up the most fuss get the best treatment. *Squeaky wheels get the oil*, as my old mentor used to say.

The labour continues to progress normally, contractions speeding up and the cervix a little more dilated. I leave Leah bouncing on the birthing ball under the supervision of her midwife. I'm not supposed to leave the birth suite, but I ignore the resistance. I slip the stethoscope on over the scrubs. I'm in full doctor-incognito mode now. They have the names of the junior doctors on call written on the whiteboard. First and second names, thankfully. Tom Ruddle, a male doctor, is the paediatrics doctor on call.

There is a hospital phone on the wall beside the lift. I dial zero for the switchboard.

"Hello, this is Dr Tom Ruddle, the paediatrics doctor on call. Can you put me through to Dr Sheehan, Consultant Obstetrician? This is an emergency – one of his patients has arrived."

"Just a moment, please."

The hospital phone connects me to a mobile.

A slightly tired-sounding voice mumbles, "Hello, this is Dr Sheehan."

"Hello Dr Sheehan, this is Dr Anthony Clooney, husband of your patient, Ms Leah Clooney. I'm just ringing to inform you that she has been admitted to the labour ward, and your presence is required."

"Who is this?"

"Dr Anthony Clooney."

"The damn shrink?"

"Well, *psychiatrist*, yes."

"How did you get my phone number?" An unexpected, wild swing from a red lightsaber.

"Via hospital switch. Are you coming in?" A heroic block with the blue lightsaber, but under pressure.

"I'm not on-call tonight." He bears down from higher ground with the full force of the dark side.

"Are you refusing to attend?" I duck and roll, and he loses the advantage of the higher ground.

"The midwives can ring me if I'm required. Up until that point, Dr Murphy is on call." He throws a safety swing to gauge the range.

"Well, what's the point of paying five grand if you're going to stay in bed?" A parry and a forceful swing from myself.

"Listen, the midwives will ring if I need to come in. See you in the morning, Dr Clooney." He dodges the swing easily, and the Dark Lord retreats.

I sneak past the midwife station and resume my post at the bedside. The water for the birthing pool hasn't been drawn yet, so it's still early doors.

At 4.30am, the junior doctor returns and does her check.

"Anything to report, Dr O'Donnell?"

"Erm, no, Mr Clooney."

"It's *Dr* Clooney."

"Sorry, Dr Clooney. Ms Clooney is doing great. The contractions are becoming more frequent, and the cervix has dilated another centimetre. Everything seems to be going well."

"When did your shift start, Dr O'Donnell?" I click the blue lightsaber on.

"I don't see how that is any of your business." She arms herself, not sure whether to attack or retreat.

"I want to know when your shift started, how many consecutive nights you've worked and how impaired your cognition might be as a result of sleep deprivation." A peppering of thrusts.

"Today is Wednesday, and it's about 4.30am. I'm doing a twenty-four-hour shift. I've been up since 9am yesterday. So, this is about my seventeenth or eighteenth consecutive hour. I wasn't on call yesterday or the day before." She blocks and retreats.

"*Maraíonn Tuirse*, Dr O'Donnell."

"Excuse me?"

"Tiredness kills."

Everything goes well, and Leah's in the pool by 7am. No epidural, a bit of gas and air. She's crowning by 7.30 a.m. and pushes the baby out. Tough as nails. No bother to her. Leah is a stickler for tradition, so she wants me to cut the cord as late as possible so that the baby can get as much maternal blood and nutrients as it can. There is no consultant of any flavour present, neither Sheehan nor Murphy. I guess they weren't needed, really. That was five grand for nothing more than reassurance.

I've planned this event meticulously for the last nine months. Well, in actual fact, a lot longer: managing jobs, promotions, house rentals, Leah's own career, her family, getting the house, the car, the buggy. But it doesn't feel real. It feels like I've ingested ketamine, and I'm watching from outside my own body. I see the paediatrics junior doctor – must be Tom Ruddle – come in and do the baby check. I see him checking notes and whispering to the nurse. I'm holding my baby. It's a boy. His name is Claude, or Luke; we actually didn't settle on a name.

I look into my baby's eyes, downward slanting. I put my finger out. I'm doing it because I've seen it in films, as well as it feeling like the right thing to do. A little hand reaches out and grabs. A single palmar crease. There is something not quite right here.

I remember the day we got the test results. We arrived at Sheehan's rooms a little early, anxious to get the results of the genetic tests, positive or negative. With our ages, we always knew a genetic disorder or a congenital problem would be a risk. We had discussed it; we both agreed it wouldn't change whether we would continue with the pregnancy or not. We just wanted to know in advance, to prepare ourselves. Standing on the step, I was about to ring the bell when the door opened and out came Kieran Cooney, of all people, wearing his Munster tracksuit, reminding everyone he is a professional rugby player. He nearly knocked me off the step. His partner followed him in floods of tears. We said nothing.

We went into Sheehan's office, and he said he had glorious news. We were all clear, a perfectly normal baby.

But now, they want to take the baby down to the neonatal unit for some extra checks. I don't want to let him go. Leah has to intervene.

Leah held the baby, and she didn't seem to notice anything. Probably all that oxytocin and skin-to-skin contact she goes on about. They pull the plug on the pool, and Leah gets into a gown. It's morning, but she's exhausted, so I let her sleep.

The midwife comes in, pushing a wheelchair.

"I'm sorry, everyone, but we need the room for another delivery."

I am about to protest, but she's already woken Leah, who seems happy to go. Leah takes a step and then vomits, first into her mask and then onto the floor. Her face drains of colour and she collapses. The midwife shouts for help. I lower her head gently to the floor; there's a pulse, but it's weak. This doesn't feel like it's happening to me. I feel like I'm watching it from the corner of the room.

The junior doctor from last night comes in and I shout at her to get the anaesthetist, the only doctor in this hospital I'd trust in an emergency. The actual emergency department is across town, but anaesthetic doctors are trained to manage the ICU. Leah isn't breathing; she looks pale blue. I start chest compressions. Everything fades into a blur. People telling me to leave, people calling security, people calling the police.

## 3rd Floor, Maternity Hospital, 24 hours later.

I am on the third floor of the hospital. It's in infrequent use, and there are no patients here. Leah is in the mortuary in the Regional Hospital across town. She never made it to the ICU. A lung clot? A brain bleed? Internal bleeding? Sepsis? Nobody knows yet.

The baby is on the ground floor in the neonatal unit. They are treating him for jaundice. It buys them time. They don't know what to do with me; the Gardaí have gone. There are two security guards at the door. It's just me and my emergency labour bag. They somehow got my swipe from me – or maybe I gave it to them. I don't remember.

I haven't slept. I haven't seen my son, and I'll never see my wife alive again. I open up the meditation app on my phone. I visualise a blue lightsaber in my mind. I repeat my mantra, "Fear is the path to the dark side. Fear leads to anger. Anger leads to hate. Hate leads to suffering."

A knock at the door. I check the app: fifteen minutes have passed. I feel cooler.

"Hello, my name is Michelle Synnott. I'm the hospital grief counsellor. Can I come in?"

She's wearing a mask. I'm seated in the hospital chair, two feet on the ground, two hands on the arms of the chair. I am cool. My phone app tells me my heart rate is 60 bpm. I slip my mask on.

"I'd like to begin by saying, I can't imagine what you're going through right now."

She's good. She knows not to imply too much, not to jump in with a sympathetic trite comment.

"Perhaps you'd like to tell me what you are feeling?"

I sit back in the chair and look at her. I give nothing away. No body language for her to mimic, no tone of voice for her to adapt to. I say nothing. I feign eye contact, and I focus on a spot just above her eyebrows but below her fringe.

"I can see you're not in the mood for talking right now. Perhaps I'll leave this with you." She puts a pamphlet on the table.

I don't acknowledge it. I'm not really here. My body, my mind, are elsewhere, weighing up where I went wrong, what I did badly, what I'd do differently the next time. My soul is not here either. It's disjointed. It's not in Heaven, because that's ridiculous, but it's somewhere in the Force, mingling with Leah's.

The counsellor leaves.

My phone tells me time passes. I'm grateful for the charger. Another knock at the door. I close off the flame, ending my meditation, and return to the room, in part.

"Hello, Dr Clooney."

"It's Mr Clooney."

"I'm sorry...?"

She pauses. Fixes her mask. She is wearing a business suit, looks like a hospital manager. She certainly isn't a nurse or a doctor.

"I'm no longer a doctor. I've resigned my post and profession."

"Okay, Mr Clooney, my apologies. My name is Chelsea Hutton, and I am the CEO of the Hospital Group. I would just like to extend my deepest sympathies to you on the passing of your wife."

I squeeze the handles of the chair. My hands go white. *Fear is the path to the dark side. Fear leads to anger. Anger leads to hate. Hate leads to suffering.*

"Thank you for your condolences."

"It's just, we feel that the maternity hospital is not the best place for you to be now."

"I want to see my son."

"Yes, we'll bring you down as soon as we can."

"I want to see my son NOW."

"We'll arrange that as soon as we can, but there are a lot of sick babies on the neonatal unit with some very tired mothers. You caused quite a bit of disruption on the labour ward earlier, but we'll…do our best."

I leap from the chair and scream into her face, "I WANT TO SEE MY SON NOW." There is no blue or red lightsaber now. It's pure, colourless hellfire radiating from the tips of my fingers and burning from my eyes. By the time she slithers away and the security guards enter, I am sitting back in my chair.

*Fear is the path to the dark side. Fear leads to anger. Anger leads to hate. Hate leads to suffering.* 120 bpm.

There are a lot of missed calls on my phone: my parents, Leah's parents, siblings, friends. Most looking for a happy update, a snap of baby and mum doing well. I haven't told anyone anything.

I eat an energy bar when the phone tells me it's 1pm. It's a nice one, with coconut. Leah's favourite.

Another knock at the door.

"Hi, Tony. It's me, James. Can I come in?"

James is a perinatal psychiatrist. He works in the maternity hospital full-time, looking after all the anxiety and depression and occasionally post-partum psychosis that comes through the door. He's a good egg. He was my senior when I was in training. I like him. He looks like even more of a psychiatrist than I do: shorter, tubbier, less hair, smaller, softer hands.

"Hi, James."

This could be a great battle of minds, like Yoda versus Darth Sidious. Instead, it's more like Obi-Wan Kenobi versus Anakin Skywalker after Anakin had his arm sliced off. I can't see any blood pouring out of me, but I can feel it oozing. I pat myself down, but my hand is dry.

He says nothing, and I say nothing.

I see his glasses fogging up and his shoulders trembling. James knew Leah well; we weren't much for socialising with other couples, but we had met with James and his wife many times. We'd also bumped into him in the clinic here. Leah liked him, which was a good sign.

"It's okay to cry. It's been a terrible shock for everyone," I say instinctively. I'm grateful for the two-metre social distancing that prevents him from giving me a hug.

After a moment, he asks, "Have you been able to get any sleep in here?"

It's a good question and a pertinent one.

"Ah, it's hard. I dozed a little in the chair, maybe six hours in total," I lie. I haven't slept since we came in.

"How's your thinking been, Tony? Are you able to make sense of any of this?"

I keep my theories about Kieran Cooney to myself.

"It's all been so sudden: the death, the Down Syndrome. My head is in such a spin," I'm not sure if James can tell I am speaking in pretend English. My mouth is on autopilot as it reflectively says things to defend itself against threats.

James continues with some banal questions, then surprises me with, "Any thoughts of harming yourself?"

I blink. "No, not at all. I have no suicidal ideation, intent, or plan." That probably set off a few alarm bells. Too robotic.

"How about thoughts of harming others?"

I vaguely recall ranting about the Freedom of Information Act, getting people struck off and perhaps, indeed, threatening to kill anyone who got in my way. This happened sometime between the paramedics loading Leah onto a trolley and the Gardaí coming in to restrain me.

"No, not at all. This has all been a terrible run of unfortunate events."

"The midwife mentioned you no longer want to be addressed as Doctor. Why is that?"

"Well, it's for a couple of reasons. I realise that I am not actually working here in any capacity, so referring to me by my professional title is probably inappropriate. I know it's a bit hasty, but being a single father of a child with special needs, I don't think I'll be able to commit to full-time clinical practice anymore. I'll ask in the University about a teaching job instead." The lies roll off my tongue.

James seems reasonably satisfied with this. He makes some small talk and looks to make an exit. Just as he is about to leave, he comes back.

"Just one more thing…."

Ah, the auld Detective Columbo double-take.

"Do you think you need a bit of a break? Somewhere quiet to go?" Detective James asks.

"Like 5b?" The name of the psychiatric ward over in the main hospital.

"I wouldn't say that. How about St John of God's or St Pat's?" Private psychiatric hospitals in Dublin.

"If I wanted to stay in a hotel, James, the Strand is across the road."

"You don't think you need psychiatric care or treatment?"

Shit, is he genuinely thinking of having me committed?

"I'd be open to the idea of treatment if it was necessary, but I don't feel I am currently suffering from a mental disorder as per the Act." The Mental Health Act; legalisation to detain people against their will on psychiatric grounds. The men in the white coats.

"I hear you, I hear you. Well, I'll check in with you tomorrow, Tony, if that's okay."

"Look forward to it. Thanks, James."

As he departs, I take out my phone and google the distance between the maternity hospital and the Northern Irish border. The Irish Mental Health Act doesn't apply in the North, and they'd have to extradite me to get me back. Three hours thirty minutes to Newry. I'd have to get my baby first.

Before I have time to craft a plan, there is another knock on the door. Two security guards flank a hospital social worker. I recognise her face despite the mask: she's originally from Australia. The epitome of social workers.

An old joke jumps into my head: *What's the difference between a social worker and a Rottweiler? At least you get a part of your kid back from a Rottweiler.*

I never expected to be on this side of the conversation.

"Hi, Dr Clooney. My name is Sheila O'Leary. We've met before. I am informing you that the hospital has sought a section 13 Emergency Court Order under the Child Care Act 1991 to keep your son in hospital until there is a safe place to discharge him to."

I grip the handles of the chair. White fire smoulders up before my eyes. I think of the blue flame. *Fear is the path to the dark side. Fear leads to anger. Anger leads to hate. Hate leads to suffering.*

"Hi, Sheila; thank you for informing me. Under the current conditions, that's probably the most sensible thing to do."

Sheila breathes a sigh of relief. The security guards seem a bit more relaxed.

"It's just temporary until we have a better understanding of everything."

"I should probably head off myself. Is it okay if I drop into the neonatal unit on my way out?"

Sheila glances at the security guards.

"You'd need to be escorted by security and see the baby with the midwives present."

"Of course."

I take my phone out: it's nearly 5 p.m.

"Dr Sheehan is due to see you as well. Maybe we could go down after that?"

"Okay, thanks, Sheila."

I visualise the blue flame. *Fear is the path to the dark side. Fear leads to anger. Anger leads to hate. Hate leads to suffering.* I check my pulse on the phone. 60 bpm.

It's 5.30 p.m. No sign of Sheehan. I have a look at the Limerick Leader site on my phone.

"Kieran Cooney – blessed by miracle," the headline reads.

I skim through the text.

"Limerick hero…Munster and Lions winger…girlfriend gave birth to third child…initially told he had a genetic disorder born perfectly normal…."

A knock at the door. In comes Sheehan, his floppy grey hair greyer than usual. He looks old. He *is* old. He's wearing a red tie…

"Mr Clooney, I'm so sorry this has all happened. You must be heartbroken."

Focus on the flame. *Fear leads to anger…*

"The hospital informs me there was an administrative error in the resulting of the prenatal testing…"

Focus on the flame. *Fear leads to anger…*

"Your late wife's test was mixed with another patient of mine. I have ordered a complete and full enquiry. Don't worry…"

I remember his fat paws labelling the specimen samples. CLOONEY and COONEY, easily confused.

Focus on the flame. *Fear leads to anger...*

"we'll do everything we can to seek justice on your behalf."

I need to get out of this room.

I pick up the emergency bag and begin gathering my things. I want to put my phone in the front pocket, but it doesn't fit. Ah, the scalpel. I remove it – I won't be needing it anymore. The screen saver flashes, and the previous browser page opens. A picture of Kieran Cooney smiling broadly with his new son. He winks at me.

"We must await the result of the post-mortem to determine what happened to your late wife. It could be a pulmonary embolism or even an amniotic fluid embolism. As you know, the chances of these things happening are infinitesimal –"

"It's called a post-mortem *examination*."

"I beg your pardon?"

"You said post-mortem. That just means 'after death'. The correct expression is post-mortem examination."

"Eh, yes, of course.... Do let me know if there is anything else I can do for you."

I unsheathe the surgical scalpel and launch myself at Sheehan.

He falls to the ground under my weight.

## Central Mental Hospital, August 2020

Afterwards, someone told me there were ninety-seven wounds on his body. I don't exactly remember. Sheehan went into cardiac arrest. He didn't reach the ICU either. I heard they're moving the maternity hospital onto the General Hospital site soon. Always a silver lining.

They send me photos of baby Luke. He is staying with a foster family. I haven't been allowed to see him. There simply isn't a precedent for this. The junior doctor on call wants to write a case report: *Post-natal Psychosis in a Father.*

I catch a glimpse of myself in the mirror. Masked up. Blue, lifeless eyes.

Am I psychotic? Am I a psychopath?

At the initial hearing, there were a lot of things in my favour: recent bereavement, new baby, new unexpected diagnosis, forty-eight hours without sleep.

All I had to say was, "Maraíonn Tuirse. Tiredness kills, a grim name for a town."

# ST MARY'S

Henry O'Connell

The cramped nurses' station was busy as always, with bells and telephones ringing incessantly and nursing staff and care attendants coming and going. Down the corridor, there was the constant noise of doors slamming, trolleys rolling, and trays banging. The whole place was too warm, and this magnified the impact of the various hospital smells, from human waste and detergent to unwanted flowers. And then there was the incessant chatter and gossip of the staff.

In the middle of the chaos, Dr Michael Carroll was trying to have a conversation with Nurse Marie Dempsey, who was in charge of the female ward for the day. He had just spent almost six hours walking the ward with her and seeing to every imaginable minor medical problem. Of course, she had skipped off on her two allocated tea breaks during that time, as always. In fact, he had been in the middle of discussing a treatment plan with her for one of the sicker patients when she took her second break; she just looked at her watch, smiled at him and walked off the ward. He had reviewed practically all of the twenty elderly female residents for numerous ailments, such as itches, insomnia and mild constipation. They all seemed vaguely familiar to him, like he had met them in previous stages of his career. He was now under pressure to get back to his practice in Dublin for the afternoon clinic. Lunch would have to be missed again, meaning he would have a headache and be irritable for the afternoon. Hunger, caffeine withdrawals and that uncomfortable fullness that comes with having no toilet break – he was becoming used to this combination of feelings after his visits to St Mary's Nursing Home.

He had taken up the role of visiting GP to St Mary's two months before. It had sounded manageable at the time. There would be a ward round every Monday from 9-11am on the female ward and the same on the male ward on Tuesdays. Then he had to be available by phone for emergencies until 5pm during the week, with an on-call doctor covering the nights and weekends. All of the patients were elderly, stable and 'long stay'. Many of them had advanced dementia. The expectation was that he would usually be treating minor ailments. He would use this clinical experience to learn more about age-related healthcare. And the steady income would be useful to boost his fledgling GP practice in the city.

It had seemed like a good idea, but things were not going well. Perhaps he should have suspected something wasn't going to go as smoothly as planned the day he met his predecessor, Dr Robert Doyle. Dr Doyle was elderly and winding down his long career. His stewardship of St Mary's was one of the last things he needed to hand over before retiring fully. There had been a strange look about Dr Doyle at their one and only meeting; a tired, suspicious and frightened look. He had given a distinctly relieved sigh as he handed over his set of keys for St Mary's.

"Any other problems then, Marie?" Dr Carroll took a deep breath as he posed this question to the nurse, trying to appear calm.

She smiled at him and looked carefully at the dusty ward book. The ward book was one of the many old fashioned devices still used in St Mary's. With her slow movements and ponderous checking of the book, he felt that she was mocking his time-pressured frustration. He started to pack away his stethoscope.

"Don't put it away yet, Doctor. I need you to see Mrs Aherne. She's in Ward 3. *Very* chesty. Your antibiotic from last week hasn't touched her."

He followed her back down the main corridor. So, she was casually criticizing his treatment again – one of her standard tactics. "Haven't we already been in Ward 3?"

"Yes, Doctor, but you didn't see Mrs Aherne, even though I did ask you."

He felt that her use of his professional title was designed to annoy him in some way. "Please call me Michael, Marie. I've said that to you before. We're colleagues."

They entered the six-bedded ward and found Mrs Aherne in the far corner beside the window. She was sleeping comfortably and looked content.

Reluctantly, Dr Carroll woke her, checked her pulse and listened to her chest. Nurse Dempsey looked on, displaying the vaguest hint of a smile.

"She seems fine to me," he said to Nurse Dempsey. "How do you feel, Mrs Aherne?"

She was clearly disorientated. She smiled at him. "I'm fine, Father. Is John gone out with the cattle?"

"There's no point in asking her how she feels, Dr Carroll. She has severe dementia; don't you remember from last week? And there must be something wrong with that stethoscope of yours, because she's definitely brewing a pneumonia."

Dr Carroll smiled and shook Mrs Aherne's hand. His frustration was building, but he would swallow it down, as usual. He followed Nurse Dempsey back to the nurses' station.

"Well?" she said, placing her hands on her hips. "Will you write her up for an antibiotic?"

"I don't think she needs one," he said, feeling increasingly hot and frustrated at her undermining of his judgement.

"Can't you write it up, and we'll use it if she gets

worse? It's just that we'll have to get the on-call doctor out later tonight. And we don't like doing that, as he's always so busy. He's excellent, and I know he'd put her on an antibiotic straightaway."

Dr Carroll took a deep breath and smiled. He had promised himself that he would not get into any more upsetting arguments with the nurses at St Mary's. He looked around the nurses' station at the old-fashioned fixtures: an ancient typewriter in the corner, the ink bottles on the shelves, and large musty logbooks stacked up to the ceiling. St Mary's Hospital had been a private mansion before being converted into a nursing home in the 1930s. Entering the hospital felt like going back in time. Since starting to provide medical cover here, he had begun to dread the Monday and Tuesday morning round with the nurses. The rounds were always longer than initially agreed. He started earlier than nine, but he could never finish before two. The nurses didn't seem to trust him. They didn't seem to understand him. They didn't even seem to have heard of the medications he prescribed.

He tried to think of Jenny, his girlfriend. She was coming back tonight. She had been in England with her family for Halloween, and he had missed her. She was also his GP colleague, so he had missed her at work, too.

"Think of me," she would breathe into his ear whenever he started to complain about St Mary's. "If you have a bad time there, I'll make it up to you that night." At this, she would kiss him gently on the lips and give him an exaggeratedly lustful wink as she pulled away. God, he missed her. He imagined her face, and he could almost smell her hair, her perfume, her breath.

On the issue of the antibiotic for Mrs Aherne, he decided to make a compromise. "I'll write it up provisionally, but I don't want her to have it unless she starts to have significant symptoms. Watch her physical observations every four hours: temperature, pulse, respiratory rate. Call me before five this evening if she seems unwell."

He noticed the nurse smile to herself and clenched his jaw.

"That's fine, Doctor."

"Anything else, then?" he asked, glancing quickly at his watch. The afternoon clinic was going to be busy. Jenny being off for the week meant he had to deal with everything. He had fifteen patients booked in, with the chance of a few emergencies too. The clinic started at 2pm. It would take him twenty minutes to drive back to the city. It was now 1.50pm, so he was already late. He felt a brief horrible flush of anxiety and pinpricks of sweat on his forehead and back. He hated being late. He always thought being late made a doctor seem unprofessional.

"Well, Doctor, I could have you here trying to deal with problems all day," she said, looking slowly through the musty ward-book. "But I don't think we're going to solve anything else right now. I can see you want to get to your lunch."

"No lunch for me today, Marie – or most days, for that matter. I'm already late for my clinic in town," he said, quickly and angrily.

They walked down the main corridor in silence and stopped at the front door.

"Time management is something you need to work on, Doctor," trilled Marie.

He felt another quick flush of anger and anxiety. He tried to distract himself by looking at the detail of the stained glass in the front door. "Well, I've been here since eight this morning. You've had two breaks in that time. I've had none."

"Now, Doctor," she smiled. "We said we wouldn't quarrel after last week."

"Yes, that's right. I apologise," he said, even though he had to force the words out in reluctant surrender. He thought of Jenny again and felt a little calmer. The wet October day outside already looked half-dark. "Speaking of last week," he said, "I'm assuming Mrs Doran has improved?"

"Well, Doctor, she is no longer suffering. She died the day after you saw her and prescribed that medication."

He thought this was a bad joke for a brief moment, but the nurse didn't crack a smile. "She died? Why didn't you call me?!" he demanded.

"We have a protocol whereby we must inform the regular doctor, yourself, up to 5pm or the on-call doctor after-hours, as you well know, doctor. She died at midnight. Should I call you again in future? I wouldn't like to be interrupting your social life," she was smiling again. She was hammering home these protocol details to him with relish. And yet she would not answer his question – why had they not called him? *Whatever the time of day*, he thought to himself, *Mrs Doran was my patient and I should have been informed, regardless of protocol.*

"Of course I would like to be informed. I knew Mrs Doran very well, and I'd been treating her for her heart failure for the past four weeks."

She looked at him blankly. "Your treatment wasn't…well…enough." She feigned an embarrassed look. "The doctor on-call was a little surprised at the medications you had used for her. I won't say what he said, exactly." She looked at the floor.

"What did he say?" Dr Carroll almost shouted, walking blindly into one of her characteristic traps. He doubted himself for a second. Maybe he *had* missed something.

"Oh now, Doctor, calm yourself! I don't mean to cause any trouble. He simply said that he wasn't surprised that she was dead, with the medication you had her on."

Dr Carroll glanced over her shoulder at the old clock, curling and uncurling his fists as he took deep breaths in time with the second hand. It was 2pm. He knew that the first few patients would already be sitting in his waiting room in the city. Being late would affect his reputation and his ability to build up a practice. But this nurse had just accused him of mismanaging the care of a patient, of killing an elderly lady. She had done it indirectly, as always.

2pm. There was no time for this now. He felt weak with hunger. He had that heavy cotton-wool feeling in his head that he got with caffeine withdrawal. The anger and frustration of the morning were building and expanding in his chest, threatening to spill out. He had never been accused of anything like this, not even in this place. "Please ask that doctor to call me at my clinic. I wish to discuss his comments with him."

Another smile from the nurse. "If that makes you feel better, Doctor."

Dr Carroll ran across the gravelled car park and jumped into his car, throwing his bag into the passenger seat: 2.03pm. He would be half an hour late now. He sped out of the car park and down the long, narrow, tree-lined lane that led from St Mary's to the main Dublin road. He felt sick to his stomach. *Poor Mrs Doran*, he thought. He knew he had done everything correctly. He had seen her the previous Monday. She had smiled at him and told him he was very young to be a doctor. He met with her husband and told him about her condition and how he was confident that she would be fine. Her husband had seemed reassured by this: "Well, you're the doctor, sir!"

He picked up speed along the lane. A fox darted into the ditch. It was nearly dark enough for a fox to be out prowling, yet it was still the middle of the day. After a mile, he was at the junction with the main road and indicating to turn right into the city. His breathing was starting to return to normal. Half an hour late was not too bad, after all. Doctors got delayed all the time for emergencies – he couldn't exactly have left when there was a patient in need. But he had to talk to that doctor who had made the accusation about his care for Mrs Doran. He was sure he'd done everything correctly. But he would have to check his notes in detail and write a report.

His mobile phone rang. It was Nurse Dempsey again. He felt another horrible flash of anger mixed with anxiety. This was something she often did. She would keep him on the ward until she knew he was late for his clinic and then call him for something else before he had got into the city.

"Yes, Marie? Has something happened?" he said in a clipped voice, trying to control the tone as he pulled the car up onto a grass verge. He looked helplessly at the clock on his dashboard.

"Mrs Aherne has spiked a temperature, so I'm starting that antibiotic. And I need you to come back immediately to see another lady. Mrs Phelan has chest pain, and I think it could be cardiac in origin. And I think they need you on the male ward after that. There's a few there that are not well today. I know you're not usually on the male ward until Tuesday, but these problems can't wait."

He thought for a second that she must be joking. He put the phone on loudspeaker, turned the car violently and headed back up the lane.

"And the nurses are not happy with the way you spoke to me this morning. I've arranged an urgent meeting for you with the Matron at 4pm."

He didn't trust himself to speak. Accelerating sharply, he made the short journey he had just completed in reverse and parked in the spot he had started out from just five minutes before, his rear wheels churning up the gravel in frustration.

He took some more deep breaths before he got out of the car. He had years of clinical experience and training, he reminded himself. He was a young, happy, confident and effective doctor: never a single complaint in the decade since he had qualified. He had never worked in a place like St Mary's – there were bound to be some teething problems and adjustments as he got used to it.

He sat back and thought of Jenny. She would be home in six hours. They would have dinner, drink wine, talk and laugh about it all. His whole body seemed to unclench as he remembered the sweet tang of her perfume. He took another deep breath.

He could not resign his post here. He had never failed in a post. He had never failed at anything. He had worked in some of the biggest and busiest hospitals in Ireland, the UK and the US. He would not give in to St Mary's or to Nurse Dempsey.

There was a shift inside him and he took a deep breath. He took out his mobile phone again and called the practice, asking his secretary to cancel all of the afternoon appointments. He asked her to apologise to his patients, but to explain that he had to spend the rest of the day here to attend to an emergency. Between him and his secretary, he was finally going to sort this place out. He was taking control now.

He reached for his bag and retraced his steps back towards the front door of the hospital. He made himself think of Jenny again: her blue eyes, her smile, her suggestive winks, the sound of her mischievous laugh. He put his key in the door and found he could not open the lock. It made no sense. He had just locked this door behind him a few minutes before. He rattled the key around. Nothing.

Bending down, he squinted through the keyhole and jolted as he saw an eye looking back at him. He almost fell backwards in shock. The door was opened from inside, and Nurse Dempsey was standing in front of him, her arms folded. She was smiling a critical, disapproving smile.

"I've also brought in Mrs Doran's husband and sons to see you. I told them what you did to her. They are very angry."

Dr Carroll pushed past her into the main corridor, his pulse pounding in his ears. How could she think this was acceptable? It was highly unusual behaviour, even for her. But, to his astonishment, there they were in the corridor, Mr Doran, crying, with three middle-aged sons gathered around, all of them looking at Dr Carroll with venom.

"You killed our mother," one of them shouted.

Then Dr Carroll had a horrible, creeping realisation that *maybe* every patient in St Mary's was someone he had failed to save at some stage in the past. Maybe it was Mrs Doran's son's voice and his accusing tone that brought the memories back. He remembered Mrs Doran from before. He had spent weeks trying to figure out how he had lost her. And now he had lost her again. Maybe he was even negligent and had been responsible for her death.

He turned to look at the nurse. She was still smiling, her head bowed. He could hold back no longer. She had tortured him for six hours already today, on the pretence of a ward round. She had accused him of malpractice. Now she had lied to this unfortunate family and turned them on him.

"You bitch," he heard himself shout at her.

She stopped smiling and moved slowly backwards.

He reached for her. "You bitch, you lying evil bitch!" He reached for her again and caught her this time, both of his hands firmly on her throat. He squeezed. The more he squeezed, the worse he felt. His head felt full, like it was about to burst. Then he was choking. And she was starting to smile again. She seemed completely unaffected by his hands squeezing on her throat. He squeezed tighter, and her smile stretched into an eerie grin. Because it was *he* who was choking. His throat was dry and hot. He could not breathe or shout or stop the feeling. He felt Mr Doran and his sons pull at him from behind. Then they were punching him in his ribs and back. And Nurse Dempsey started to laugh.

\*\*\*

Dr Jenny Ryan's plane touched down in Dublin at 7pm, as planned. She had missed Michael over the past week. And she knew he had missed her. He'd sounded tired and stressed whenever they spoke on the phone. They would relax tonight. A week apart was always tough, but the reunions were great. And things were looking up for them: the practice was starting to pay for itself, and they were starting to feel settled in the city. Another year and he would be able to give up that awful position at St Mary's. It sounded like a terrible place to her. She had never visited or seen it, but he had told her all about it; the old-fashioned interiors, the endless minor ailments, the undermining nurses, the monotonous and pointless ward rounds and the subsequent time pressures on their practice in Dublin. Whenever they talked about St Mary's, he wound himself up until his stories turned into furious rants and sweat beaded on his forehead. Before she had left to visit her family, they had agreed to stop talking about the place altogether.

She moved quickly from the plane to baggage collection and passed swiftly through passport control. The airport was quiet. She turned on her phone as she approached arrivals. She would check it in the taxi. Michael would be home by now. She could ring him on the way.

She rang three times on the taxi journey, but he did not answer. He wasn't at the apartment when she got there, and again, there was no answer on his phone. Jenny felt a deep dread in the pit of her stomach that she couldn't explain. She instinctively thought of St Mary's. Michael would have had a shift there that day.

An hour later, she was growing increasingly frantic, pacing up and down the hallway of their flat. The doorbell rang and Jenny wrenched it open.

Her knees buckled when she saw two Gardaí at the door.

They eased her into the flat, lowered her onto the sofa, gently forced a glass of water into her trembling hands. And then they explained how Michael's body had been found hanging in the derelict remains of an old mansion belonging to the Fitzroy family, a few miles from the city. It had been used as a Voluntary Aid Detachment hospital during the First World War but had remained empty and disused since then.

St Mary's nursing home had never existed.

# THE LOST DOCTOR

## Frank McKenna

Professor Chris Devlin stands half-hidden behind the podium. The projected black screen above his left shoulder reads, in giant white Arial font: "Questions?"

He nods at the gangly, self-assured Jenny Grover in the front row with her hand in the air.

"I'm sorry, I don't understand," she says and shrugs.

Hands in the air used to be a good thing. It meant students were engaged. But somehow, over the last few months, they had become threats. Missiles, trained on his failing self and on his specialty. Where he used to pluck those missiles out of the air and disarm them, retrain them, such powers had abandoned him to torture behind enemy lines. The questions at the end of class – *when that bloody slide comes up* – they're the ones that irk the most. Class was over. Ceasefire has been declared. Further shots are just…vindictive.

"What do you not understand?" he asked.

Jenny Grover was aghast. "How can you say this person has an illness? Just because they don't behave as you think they *should*. Psychiatrists are not...." She trailed off.

For Devlin, she is the worst type of medical student. The ones who come bubbling with agenda. The ones who arrive on their psychiatry rotation, laden with preconceptions, misconceptions, tainted by their own unsatisfactory experiences. They come believing psychiatry is a joke, a pseudoscience, where diagnoses cannot be confirmed by a level in the blood or an anomaly on a scan; where a doctor's skill is perceived as more nebulous.

Devlin understands their doubts. He lives in the world they live in. But he has also seen what they have not and knows that truth traverses the doctrines and anti-doctrines.

He used to be up for the fight, professionally speaking. He could recall conversations with the Dean, with the Head, where he had spoken with passion and anger and optimism.

*The curriculum needs to change. These future doctors need, more than any knowledge, to be able to sit with patients and not run from the malaise or obsession or delusion they are presented with. To see that psychiatric patients are not...other.*

Sharing that, explaining that, is why he decided to teach. How noble and foolish to desire to clarify truth.

He used to be good at it, though. At least, he *thinks* he was. It's so vague now. It's hard to see himself ever having been competent or ever being competent again. And yet, *Thank You* cards adorn the shelves in his office; from students – sceptical students, students who had been like Jenny Grover, whose course it seemed he had managed to retrain.

But he was a fool. The minor victories of years past are meaningless. They are outliers. The cards are tokens of appreciation of effort, not of accomplishment or progress. His clinical psychiatric colleagues continue to complain of the understandably sad or the antisocial patients that their medical and surgical counterparts refer to them, of how their patients are shooed out the door by other specialties. Devlin has inspired no one.

For months now, he's been waking before five, unable to find sleep again. He lies on his back, palms upturned to the ceiling. Supine. Trying to be mindful.

Earlier this morning, in the haze of his thoughts, he vaguely foresaw a moment like this, as a weight of dread pressed him deeper into the mattress.

Eyes are on him. Even those uninterested are becoming interested – not in the answer to a fundamental question about psychiatry, but in the drama of his awkward silence, and his flustered, reddening face.

Drumming begins in his chest, vibrating through him. He feels the tingle of sweat glands activating on his forehead.

"Psychiatrists are not...?" he asks, compelling Jenny Grover to land her strike. He has a faint hope his stand might seem clever or expose some error in her thinking he cannot yet put his finger on. He is too old to be thinking this way.

There is something in his throat. He tries to clear it with a grunt. Unsuccessful, he grunts again, harder.

"Everyone is different," says the student. "They feel and experience different things. How can a psychiatrist – how can *anyone* – say there is something wrong with them? You're saying something's an illness because it's not *normal*."

This old chestnut.

He looks at his watch: no escape there. He used to struggle not to run over on this lecture. He used to revel in the battle, the reframing, the sharing of his straightforward, palatable interpretation of one of psychiatry's most controversial topics: *personality disorders*. Now, he is finishing – or trying to finish – twenty minutes early because he just can't take any more. He wipes the sweat from his brow and immediately feels the arrival of replacement beads.

He is not sure if he can speak. His voice whimpers beneath whatever is caught in his throat. He coughs harder. He begins to choke.

"Well," he manages, "I agree, everyone is different." Short sentences are key. Cough. He just needs to get this out, then he's done. "We all have traits in our personality. We might be introverted or extraverted, impulsive or contemplative. We might be agreeable or argumentative. There are many traits we can look at to paint a picture of someone's personality." He forces a long, slow exhale, trying to quell the escalating autonomic response. "But people with personality disorders come to psychiatrists because they are in distress. Because their personality continually causes problems for them and the people around them."

"But it's just…who they are. And psychiatry is calling it an illness. Psychiatry is *labelling* it."

He wonders why this is happening. He wonders why he has become so impotent. He feels things are *unfair*, something he has never allowed himself to feel.

He knows certain things. There was his divorce. His grandfather's *nerves*. The relatively recent decision to finish actually seeing patients and focus entirely on teaching – he had not foreseen the magnitude of that decision. These are things that, if present in a patient sitting in front of him, he would jot down as factors predisposing them to their depression, precipitating their depression. But this was not a patient. This was him, and such a casual, abstract formulation now seemed so inadequate.

"This patient," he says, gesturing at the screen, "is tortured. He is continually sabotaging his life, his ambitions, his possibilities for happiness." He tries hard to keep the desperation from his voice, to hold off the certainty that his words will be insufficient, that his powers of articulation, of persuasion, have long-since departed. "He thinks of killing himself, constantly."

Jenny Grover hesitates. She looks uncertain. "But, does that not mean he's depressed?" she asks.

Devlin's legs feel weak. He has no more. No fight. No courage. No response. He manages to shake his head, unable to look at Jenny Grover, unable to believe how bizarre and pathetic he must appear. He retreats to the podium, white flag dropped to the floor.

Thankfully, Jenny Grover does not pursue. The class is deathly silent.

He presses Esc on the keyboard to exit the presentation, then clicks the X to close it down. It takes its time. His heart thumps in his ears. His eyes sting with sweat.

The students bustle about with their chairs and laptops and coffee cups. The computer finally begins to shut down, and he makes for the door.

A few students have already left, and he sweeps out behind them, not meeting eyes, not even seeing clearly. He has just to cross the corridor to his office and close the door behind him, allowing this onslaught to pass.

His vision blurs around the periphery, a circle of watery movement around a focus of clarity. The focus shrinks onto the office door, then further, so that all he can see is the handle. His chest burns. He knows what this is. It's happened before. It happened before he decided to stop seeing patients…but it *might* be his heart. He *might* be about to die.

He fumbles the key out of his pocket, and it falls, clattering at the foot of his office door. He hunkers down, one hand on his chest, the other sweeping, hoping to latch onto the keys.

"Dr Devlin?"

He closes his eyes and tries to take in slow, silent breaths, trying to control his diaphragm, sucking the air in and letting it seep back out.

"Dr Devlin, are you okay?"

He presses his hands against the floor, pushing himself up, then uses the door to steady himself as he rises to his feet.

"Can I have a word?"

Devlin scans the student for a face. Vaguely familiar. Was this boy even one of his students? The name Simon comes to him. Simon S- something. Things are piecing together somewhere in his shaken mind.

"In private?" the student asks, nodding to the door.

Devlin hopes the key will slot straight in, but it takes a few seconds.

Once they are sitting, Devlin waits, fearing the worst, clueless as to what *the worst* might be.

Simon S- begins to squeeze one thumb in the fist of his other hand, twisting it, tautening the skin. His hands fold around each other and wrestle, grasping and releasing, grasping and releasing. *Wringing* is the term. Oddly, the boy wrings them in front of his face, hiding behind them. His eyes burn into the desk until they suddenly jolt up.

"I need your help," the student says.

Devlin becomes aware of the saliva collected on his tongue. He tries to keep from gulping.

"What is it, Simon?"

The student scrunches up his forehead. He briefly stops the wringing and lowers his hands. "My name is Stephen," he says.

Devlin wipes his brow again, though it makes little difference. He wants to be anywhere else. Actually, no. He wants to be in bed, curled up, duvet pulled over him, forgotten.

"I'm really sorry, Stephen. Please, tell me."

*Please,* he thinks. *Please, don't tell me.*

Stephen stands and begins to pace in the small office, zig-zagging on the carpeted floor – the rough, grey carpet that the building management feel warrants the abundant 'No food or drink' signs on the hallway walls. Devlin looks at the three empty coffee cups on his table and the stains beneath them. He has been spilling a lot recently.

"I need to drop out," says Stephen, clenching his fists into his hair and squeezing his eyes shut.

Devlin tries to compile some picture of Stephen before today; how he answered questions, what he was like in roleplays, anything about the quality of his case histories. Had Devlin really missed this distress simmering in his class? He couldn't even remember eye contact with this boy before. But most of his recent students blurred together. Each face was a moveable fragment of the classroom, each written case history a blade of grass in an overgrown meadow of Times New Roman font.

Devlin asks why.

"Isn't it obvious?" Stephen's eyes shoot open, bloodshot and moistened, firing panic across the desk. "Please! Don't pretend you don't know!"

"You've been doing fine," says Devlin. "You're a bit quiet in class, but –"

"My face!" Stephen shouts. "My nose!" He points his finger in demonstration before cupping his nose in his hand and turning away, a sob exploding from between his fingers.

"What's wrong with your nose?" *There's nothing wrong with your nose.*

"Oh, come on!"

Devlin sits a little straighter. He watches as Stephen forces his hands slowly down but, before they pass his neck, they return to his face – covering, protecting.

"Really, I don't know," says Devlin. But he thought he might.

Even with his recent decline, Devlin would have known this boy's face, surely. He would have held his gaze at some point and found some sense of him.

No, this boy had been invisible. This boy had been hiding.

"Please," says Stephen. "You're a doctor. I know you're my teacher, but you're still a doctor. Please don't pretend. I'm sick of people pretending. I can't stomach it."

It is a subtle thing that shifts inside Devlin, but later, he will know that it has happened. He feels some of what Stephen feels. It traces in his matter. He recalls this sense of empathy that had somehow absconded, diffused in the scales of a serpent that had constricted him. The sense that has always been core. Core to his psychiatric nebula.

He Devlin takes a coffee-stained napkin from the table and wipes his forehead again, though this time, the sweat does not replace so quickly. He watches the young man across the desk continue to pace, and there is a loosening across Devlin's chest. His shoulders seem to pull back a little, all by themselves. He feels calm.

"Okay," he says, gesturing for Stephen to retake his seat. "Tell me, in your words, what it's like for you."

# A Letter to Dr Conolly Norman

Henry O'Connell

Dr James Ryan
Davin's Guesthouse
O'Connell Street
Clonmel
Co. Tipperary

*22nd June, 1895*

Dr Conolly Norman
Resident Medical Superintendent
Richmond District Lunatic Asylum
Dublin

Dear Dr Norman,

I hope this letter finds you well. As you can see from the above address, I am writing to you from deepest Tipperary! And as I write from this small guesthouse room in the fading summer daylight, I am starting to wonder how I ever came to be here and get myself in such a quandary that I felt compelled to ask for your advice.

As you may know, I was appointed as a dispensary doctor in County Clare a few years back, and I've been soldiering away there ever since. As my wife Mary is from Lisdoonvarna and her family still lives in the surrounds, the location of my employment is not as inhospitable as it may sound. Our children are growing fast and, at times, speaking with the western brogues of their school friends!

It seems like a lifetime now since I had the privilege of working under your guidance at the Richmond Asylum. You may remember, I had at that stage an interest in following in your footsteps and becoming an alienist of some description, and you proved to be an inspirational teacher and guide to me. Then I met Mary, and the west called to her, so I ended up here in the Dispensary of Ennistymon.

The reason I am writing to you out of the blue after so many years is to ask your professional opinion on a most complicated matter. You may have already read about the man down here in Tipperary by the name of Cleary, who it is alleged to have burned his wife for a witch. The newspapers are making hay from the story, and I believe news of the scandal has actually reached as far as London and New York!

I will outline the story to you in the most concise and clinical terms; along the lines in which you taught me to communicate when we used to walk the long corridors of the Richmond together.

Michael Cleary is now aged thirty-five years, and his trade is that of a cooper. His wife, Bridget, was aged twenty-six years at the time of her death last March; she worked as a dress-maker and milliner. They had been married for seven years, though they were childless and relatively prosperous in comparison to their rural neighbours. They lived with her father in a small stone cottage in the townland of Ballyvadlea, between the villages of Cloncen and Drangan.

It appears that the poor woman had been unwell for a few weeks prior to her death, with bronchitis and fever. Relatives said that she was at times 'raving' or confused. The husband went to great lengths to help her, seeking out the local doctor on a number of occasions and then, in desperation, seeking help and remedies from local herbalists. He had Mass said in the house. Such was his dedication to helping his wife that he did not even attend the funeral of his own father a week or so before her death.

Cleary was not sleeping and losing weight and condition in his efforts to care for his ailing wife. He finally enlisted the help of her father and cousins to administer the herbal concoctions in the days before her death.

There followed several days of agony for Bridget Cleary, with her husband and relatives forcing on her the concoctions of the local herb doctor. Needless to say, the remedies did nothing to help her. The upshot was that it is claimed that Mr Cleary burned her alive in their cottage on around the 15th of March this year by holding her over her own hearth while the others looked on. Along with the couple, present in the cottage at the time of her death were also her father, her aunt and a number of her first cousins. None of the others, including Cleary himself, were harmed.

At first, she was declared to be missing, but her wretched burned corpse was found in a shallow grave near the cottage on the 22nd of March.

I have been following the story in the newspapers over the summer for a number of reasons.

Firstly, I thought it unusual that so many people would be in the house at the time of her death and, as the court hearing is proceeding, they seem to have so little to recount and report. Cleary himself is the chief suspect, of course.

Secondly, as I have described, it has been reported in court and in the newspapers that Cleary was acting very strangely in the week or two before his wife's death. As mentioned, he was not sleeping, and he had lost weight. But the eeriest thing of them all is that he was apparently making claims that his wife was not, in fact, his wife at all, but a changeling left by the fairies.

Thirdly, in the days immediately after her death, Cleary made no secret of going to an ancient ringfort nearby (such forts are believed by the country people to be residences of the fairy folk, as you may know) where he waited for three nights in succession to catch his wife on her return to the land of the living and pull her from the back of a fairy's horse!

Finally, my interest in the story is also related to my personal connections with this area. My own father came from a small farm just outside Clonmel and moved to Dublin when he was aged fourteen years. He never lost the Tipperary accent, and I visited the old homestead with him a few times before he died. Reading the accounts and the language of the witnesses reminded me of the way my father and his brothers used to speak and thus drew me in to the story further.

As with so many things in this old country, the story is being spun in different ways depending on what side of the fence you call home. In particular, the more unionist-leaning newspapers – and the English ones – are describing the story with a mixture of mirth and horror, and as final proof that the Irish are too superstitious and ignorant to ever be fit to rule themselves.

Whatever the truth of what happened, there was one particular newspaper article that grabbed my attention back in April and prompted me to take the first steps to get involved in the case. I still have the cutting here beside me, so I will quote to you directly the lines from *United Ireland*, 13th April edition, that got me thinking:

*The principal prisoner, the husband, made a statement contradicting Mrs Burke as to his throwing paraffin on the victim, denying it was his wife he put on the fire, and accusing her relatives of causing dissension and unhappiness in their conjugal relations.*

The words that grabbed me were: 'denying it was his wife he put on the fire'. What a strange thing to say! If Cleary was trying to avoid the hangman's rope, wouldn't he be better to implicate the whole lot of them in her death? The fact that he admitted to putting her on the fire but said that it was not, in fact, *his wife* he did this horrific thing to got me thinking that perhaps an assessment of his mental state was called for.

I had noticed that his barrister was a Dr John Boursiquot Falconer, a name that one would not easily forget. Falconer and I had knocked around together in Dublin during our bachelor days, and we were quite friendly at one stage. So, I wrote to him, outlining my clinical experience at the Richmond under your expert guidance, and suggested that I meet with Cleary and see what I could make of him. I offered my services without a fee. Boursiquot duly agreed, and so I arrived at Clonmel jail this morning on a mission!

I realise that I have perhaps got carried away by the fantastical events of this story. So now, I will attempt to pull myself in and get back onto the style and mode of your former student. Let me try – once again – to describe my findings in a succinct and clinical manner, as you taught me so well to do.

I arrived at the jail at ten in the morning and interviewed Cleary in a small holding cell. He is taller than the average countryman, at 5 feet 10 inches. His current weight is 154 pounds, and he told me that he has lost significant weight in recent weeks. His physical examination was unremarkable. He seems to be a strong, fit, healthy man.

He was wearing a tired grey tweed suit and work boots. His hands and fingernails were dirty, and he was in need of a shave. He is a handsome-looking man with regular features, blue eyes and fair hair that is going light on top.

He was calm and polite for the duration of our time together, despite the number of questions and the repetition of my queries. He regarded me with an air of respect, I dare say. At the outset, I told him that I hoped to be able to help him, but he did not seem to be too moved or impressed by this. In fact, he seemed to be resigned to whatever fate might lie in store for him. At one stage, he said coolly, "If I do not get justice here, I will get it in heaven."

I made sure to take my time and every care in eliciting a *clear* and *accurate* history from him. I noted that it was just gone midday when we finished our interview.

Overall, I would say that he was exhausted-looking and, had it not been for my prompting, questions and note-taking, I think he would have had very little to say to me. This was not because of intimidation or undue humility, as we so often see in the poor and the rural people, but because, I believe, he is still consumed with thoughts about his wife returning.

He confirmed with me the chronology of events as reported in court and in the newspapers.

He told me on a number of occasions that he was exhausted and deprived of sleep for weeks leading up to his wife's death because of his efforts to help her.

I will now relate to you directly some quotations from Cleary:

"Bridgie got suddenly sick with a raging pain in her head that lasted two weeks."

"I tended to her wants night and day until I was, in a manner, just as bad as her."

He told me about Jack Dunne, an older relative of his wife and someone who was well versed in the ways of fairy folklore:

"It was Jack Dunne that started it. He told me, 'Tis not Bridgie you have there but an oul' witch left behind by the fairies.'"

No matter how many times, or in what way I asked him, Cleary came back solemnly to the statements above, there or thereabouts.

In comparison to some of the unfortunate creatures I saw in the Richmond with your good self, Cleary seemed to me like a sane man in all ways apart from his notions about his wife. He did not seem to have the cloud of melancholia hanging over him or influencing his view of events. I asked him in what must have been twenty different ways about other abnormalities of the mind that I had experience of from the Richmond, and he denied them all, giving me a look at one stage to suggest that, in suggesting such lunacy, I was in fact *myself* half-touched!

The only other consistent finding I could establish was that he was convinced that Jack Dunne, Bridgie's own father, and her cousins had got together to set him up. He was consistent and convincing on this latter point, looking straight at me and repeating the words:

"That lot drove me to it. And now, where is poor Bridgie gone to?"

Towards the end of our meeting, I started to search my mind for more questions. I even went as far as imagining, in an effort to stretch my mind, that you were waiting in your office for me, waiting for me to give you a presentation and diagnosis of all I had assimilated!

Despite my intentions to be objective, I started to think that if only I could establish insanity with a few arrow-like questions that you might ask yourself, then I might be able to provide a report to his barrister that could save Cleary from the noose. Even now, as I write these words, I realise that I did not approach the interview with the professional objectivity I intended.

In fact, I had weeks ago developed the notion that

Cleary was insane and not in control of his actions when he killed his wife, and so my interview was merely a means to prove myself right. Had I been truly objective, I should have also been considering that Cleary might have been feigning insanity or even using the old piseogs of rural Ireland to excuse his heinous act.

I think I may be on Cleary's side, so to speak, because his life story and his place of residence brought to mind the place whence my father had come. Meeting with Cleary somehow convinced me that he was not a malign or dangerous man, whatever his actions back in March. My visceral senses told me that I was safe in that small cell with Cleary and that he would never again do anyone any harm unless his mind became unbalanced, as it had been for those few tragic days.

So I will leave you with these last questions.

Is it possible that the beliefs in fairy folk, as still seen in so many country people, could be powerful enough to drive a previously harmless and law-abiding man to kill his wife?

Or is it possible that Cleary's beliefs about his wife were well above and beyond the normal fairy beliefs and superstitions and were, in fact, aspects of some kind of temporary insanity? (Regarding this latter point, I am especially mindful of your paper in the *Dublin Journal of Medical Science* in 1890 on 'acute confusional insanity').

Or is it possible that I have been hoodwinked by the calm and gentle demeanour of this man and his similarities to my own dear, deceased father? Am I blinded by my own biases and simply unable to see him as a heartless and cruel killer?

As for the other individuals involved, I cannot speak for them, and I am unlikely to interview them. But I wonder if, in the tumult of this poor woman's final illness, the crowded nightly vigils at her home, the intense and close relationships between them all and the pervading mystical and superstitious beliefs that at least some of them share, could it be that the whole sorry group developed some kind of shared insanity that was perhaps started off by the ramblings of Jack Dunne and added to by the increasing desperation of Michael Cleary?

You may never have the time to read or respond to this letter. However, I assure you that having you in my mind this morning while interviewing Cleary was in itself a great assistance to me. A true mark of a great medical teacher is that his voice and reasoning is forever instilled in the mind of his student.

And writing this letter with you as the intended recipient has also helped me to bring some shape to my thinking on this sorry tale.

I will not commit my final diagnosis here, although I am certain now of my conclusion. Instead, I will leave the ending open and look forward to your response.

In any event, I know that the final verdict on Cleary will be made by Justice William O'Brien and not by a medical man. I will write to my old friend Falconer and hope that he can bring my humble findings to the attention of Justice O'Brien.

Finally, I hope that you, your family and all the staff and patients of the Richmond are doing well. I wish you every good fortune for the future, and thanks for the kindness and guidance that you gave so readily to me when I was a green and innocent young doctor all those years ago. Truly, your voice and your wisdom are always with me.

As I sign off, I can hear that the news of this case is not just in the newspapers of Dublin, London, and New York, but that it has also reached the little children of Clonmel. Right outside my window now, I hear a gang of them playing noisily and singing a newly minted skipping rhyme:

*Are you a witch or are you a fairy,*
*Or are you the wife of Michael Cleary?*

*Your student always,*
*Dr James Ryan*

# MILLIE

Frank McKenna

Millie turned right onto the footpath. Now she could really pick up speed. She dipped her head and tilted forward, spinning her legs. The gale howled around her, burning her ears as she tried to outrun it.

The pier was so wonderfully close. Far enough away that she could go full steam, but not so far that she would tire and have to slow down.

Two minutes outside was all Mum gave her. Two minutes to run and marvel at the boats and the wide-open sea before having to sit across the wooden table in the shadowed kitchen, being snapped at to eat her vegetables.

All she could think of was going faster, faster, down the hill, to see the boats.

*Careful now, Millie.* She allowed her father's voice to be swept away by the wind. She shook herself free of him and kept running.

She leapt from the footpath onto the tarmac of

the road, pumping her arms.

Then, there was a screech.

There was an explosion of energy inside her chest, bursting out through her arms and legs and fingers and toes. She hit the road and stumbled, blown sideways by the sound. A red blur filled her vision. It was the side of a car, drifting towards her, skidding as it sent gravel and small stones fizzing across her.

All Millie could do was close her eyes and wait. But the car managed to stop in time, and Millie found she was still there – ,not struck, but lying on her back with a dry layer of dust settled on her face. She squinted up at the swaying branches of a great, bare ash tree that overhung the road. Crows were cawing, having been scattered from the tree by the commotion below.

"Jesus!" A man climbed from the driver's side of the car. He rushed over and crouched in front of her, holding his hands to his head. "Are you okay?" he asked, spittle spraying from his lips and catching on the briars of his thick, black beard. "Can you hear me?" He looked at her arms and legs and at the side of his car. Then he looked up and down the street. "Where are your parents?"

Millie was silent. She felt her face reddening.

The man pushed out a loud breath and stood up straight, planting his hands on his hips. "What the hell were you doing?" he shouted. His hands were thick and dirty. His eyes were green like the sea on a dull day, flecked with dark sparks. And they were staring into her.

"Say something," he demanded.

But she didn't.

He checked up and down the road again and put a hand on his chest for a moment as he watched her sitting there. Then he turned and walked back to his car. He restarted the engine, took one more look at Millie through the car window, then turned and drove down the main street.

Millie tried to wipe dust from her tongue, but her hands and arms were dusty too. She watched the red car move quickly past the last string of buildings in the village. She expected it to then veer around the bend, out of sight, but its brake lights lit up as it slowed and turned into the pier.

Her eyes widened. She looked back towards home and waited for a moment, half expecting her mother to emerge and walk down and stand over her and grit her teeth. Millie was late for dinner. Millie had nearly caused an accident. Millie was sitting in the road, and – worst of all – Millie had a fresh graze on the side of her left knee, lightly smeared with gravel and dust-darkened blood.

*Millie?* Her father's voice was calm and kind. *Are you okay?*

She stood up and brushed herself down.

*Mum will want to clean that.*

She used her t-shirt to wipe the blood from her knee.

*Come on now, Millie. Home for dinner.*

Millie ran to the pier.

At the top of the slipway were a dozen boats, all perched on trailers, huddled together before the time came to return their bellies to the Atlantic. Millie loved to walk around them, examine their undercarriages, assess their seaworthiness. Most looked old and run-down. One or two of the wooden ones would need holes fixed before they could return to duty. But it bothered her that they sat where they did – dry, not fulfilling their purpose. If she had a boat – and when she was older, she definitely would – she would use it every day.

The tide was low. The stony pier wall was a dirty, hairy green. And there was a boat in the water! There hadn't been a boat in the water for days – a week, even. It had a red cabin and a blue metal hull. Most of the boats were a mix of red and blue.

She ran along the pier, past the pier office and alongside the boat. The tide was so low that only the tip of the boat's aerial bobbed in the air at the same height as Millie. She slowed as she approached the edge, then stopped and began tapping her foot on the concrete. She looked around and saw nobody, but there was the red car behind her. It was empty. She had run right by it and hadn't noticed. It was parked at the side of the pier office and would have been hidden from the road and the boats on the trailers as she raced along.

The man could be inside the pier office, which

was a run-down old portacabin with filthy windows you couldn't see through. Either that, or he was in the boat.

Millie moved closer to the edge.

*Careful, Millie.*

*I want to see it.*

The boat's cabin looked small, open at the back. It had two sweeping brushes pinned against its side, though looking at the deck, she imagined the brushes were hardly used. Lobster pots were stacked at one end beside a large, metal chest, and two thick blue ropes reached up from the boat, each wrapping around anchors built into the top of the pier.

There was a ladder fixed to the wall near where she stood, rising from the water next to the boat.

*No, sweetie. It's not our boat. And Mum is waiting.*

*Just for a minute?*

There was a crashing sound that almost made Millie fall off the edge, and she grabbed the top of the ladder to steady herself. It had come from the pier office. It was like something inside it had been thrown and had crashed into wooden boxes and knocked them over. Then there was more banging and crashing and sliding. He was moving things around in there, maybe looking for something, maybe cleaning it out. But he was so loud. Then she heard a soft thump, and when footsteps followed, she realised the thump had been the office door opening. He was coming.

She felt her face turn red like it did when

somebody tried to make her speak. She couldn't let him see her. She stepped over the edge of the ladder and climbed down far enough to be hidden behind the wall. When she looked down, she got a shock to see she was so high up and that the boat was not nearly as close to the ladder as she had thought.

The wall, the ladder, and the boat began to spin slowly around, and Millie's arms began to shake.

*You're okay, sweetie. Try closing your eyes.*

Millie closed her eyes. All she could feel was the grip of her hands on the ladder. Then, carried on the wind, another voice floated down and into her ears.

"Millie?" it called.

Her eyes shot open. She held her breath, waiting to hear it again, to be sure of what she heard.

"MILLIE?" There it was, louder and clearer and closer. Millie was certain. Her mother. She was there, at the pier, somewhere near the boats on their trailers. Millie squeezed tightly on the ladder and strained to look around but could not see her.

*She's going to kill me.*

*No, sweetie,* her father said. *She's certainly not going to do that.*

"Excuse me," Millie heard her mother say. "Have you seen a girl with red hair? She's eight years old."

"Sorry," said the man. "Not around here."

Millie's hands were becoming sore. The metal was cold, and she wasn't sure whether she was holding on tightly or whether her grip had become loose and might slip off altogether. She tried to squeeze harder.

She was afraid of the man seeing her and afraid that her mother would see her. She had caused her mother to come all the way from home. And now she hadn't answered when her mother had called. Sometimes, Mum got angry when she didn't answer. She wanted to answer. She always wanted to, but she just couldn't.

From above, her mother shouted her name. She sounded so cross. Nothing made Mum as cross as when Millie went missing.

"Hey!" she heard the man shout. "You can't go in there."

"I'm looking for my daughter!" her mother shouted. She sounded angry with him too, and Millie had never known her to be angry with a stranger.

There was the rumbling of movement on the soft floor inside the pier office. There was more sliding and banging and Mum's muffled shouts, calling Millie's name. The man's footsteps pounded into the office after her.

In that moment, Millie had a horrible thought that the man would hurt her mother, would perhaps *kill* her mother. And she would be dead. Just like Dad.

Millie was shaking so much it felt like she was about to break from the ladder, just snap off, and then she would fall.

*No! Don't hurt Mum!* Inside her head, there were screams. Screams that filled the air and shook the earth. She tried to squeeze the voice from her chest up to her throat and out through her mouth. She could feel her face reddening again, her neck bulging. She was like a balloon filled with too much air, about to burst.

*I'm sorry, Mummy. I shouldn't have come here. I should have done what I was told.*

There were more rushing footsteps. The lighter ones – her mother's footsteps.

"I told you, there's nobody here," said the man.

"I'm sorry," shouted her mother, but it was not an angry shout. It was different. Her voice was shaking. "My daughter. I can't…."

The shouting stopped, and hovering over the silence was the faintest sound of her mother's sobs.

Millie rested her forehead against the cold metal of the ladder, listening, barely believing, allowing the vague familiarity of her mother's crying to seep into her.

She took a deep breath in and could feel her voice building in her chest. That's the strangest thing about it – she could always *feel* her voice in there, wanting to come out. But it was trapped.

Millie pushed and pushed, but it was like there was no space for her voice to escape. Everything around her – the sea, the air, the sky, the cold – seemed to be tightening, squeezing her, choking her.

*It's okay, Millie. Try climbing up. If you climb up, Mum will see you!*

But her legs were shaking. They were trembling

so much, her knees banged off the sides of the ladder and stung with cold and pain. She was cold all over now. She didn't think she could hold on.

*Daddy!*

*It's okay, sweetie. I'm here. You're going to be okay.*

"I'm sorry," said the man. His voice was softer than before. Kinder. "I might have seen her, up at the top of the road. There was a girl. She had red hair. And freckles. Lots of freckles."

"That's Millie!"

"She didn't say her name. I tried to ask her where her parents were —"

"She doesn't speak. She hasn't spoken since her father died."

Millie's breath caught again, just for a moment. And tears came. She hadn't cried in a long time. They came, and they streamed down her face.

*Now, Millie. It's time.*

Her father's voice was calm and kind. Exactly as she remembered it. She could feel him waiting for her, knowing she would do what she didn't think she could.

She pushed her feet into the rung of the ladder, so it felt like the rung might burst out and the ladder break apart. She was still shaking, but now not with fear or cold. She felt something warm inside – hot, even – and it was going to erupt. When it exploded up through her, out came the most powerful sound she could ever imagine.

She called for her mother.

Just like that, she could breathe freely, and air flowed in and out, filling her up and bringing life to the tips of her fingers and toes. She looked up, and above the top of the ladder, at the white and fluffy white clouds that now seemed to stretch out across a vast and open sky.

Then, above her, a face appeared. It was the man, with his thick, black, wiry beard and green eyes. But they looked scared. They looked like her own must have looked when his red car was bearing down on her.

"Millie?" he asked.

She nodded. She tried again. "Yes," she said.

"Millie?" Her mother appeared beside the man.

"Mum!"

"Oh my God," said her mother. "Come up."

Millie went to say that she wasn't able, that she had been stuck and had thought she would fall. But instead, she lifted her right leg to the rung above. Then followed with her left. And she climbed, rung after rung, until helped by the man from the top and pulled into her mother's arms.

# THE EXORCISM

## Kevin Lally

I hadn't been this nervous since the first day of my medical intern year. Which, when I come to think of it, only took place twelve months ago. The nerves then were more of excited anticipation, the sweet release of a friendly dog gagging to be taken off the lead in the park. This was different. This was more of a sweaty palm, stomach-doing-somersaults type of anxiety. Maybe I should pop a propranolol – a beta blocker that calms some of the physical symptoms - or an Alprazolam – "Xanax" to the person on the street. That would make this easier.

I had been called to the headmaster's office before in school, for something puerile but forgivable. I'd been called to see the Prof Lonergan, Director of Education in medical school, the chief disciplinarian, for something slightly less puerile and slightly less forgivable. Both of which I got through relatively unscathed. Could this be worse?

I've never been summoned to the psychiatrist's

office before. A slightly conniving nurse on the ward had said something about 'erratic behaviour'. My possibly well-meaning consultant and basically my boss had suggested I take some annual leave. (It wasn't really a suggestion, more of an imperative.) A programme director had mentioned the need for an occupational health assessment prior to return. An intern co-ordinator wanted to go nuclear and demanded my case be taken to a Medical Council Fitness to Practice hearing. For now, I had dodged the guillotine, but the sword of Damocles hung very menacingly above.

Of course, I'd met psychiatrists before. I'd done clinical rotations there as a medical student, visited their wards as an intern doctor. Generally an eccentric bunch – the stereotypes not unfounded. What do they say? You can't work in a cement factory and not get dust on your shoulders? Dickie bows and brown leather elbow pads were the norm, and that's just the women.

The Department of Psychiatry is in the back of the hospital, out of sight and *almost* out of mind. Comically, it's literally in the basement of the building. I make my way through the main hospital, past the overpriced coffee shops and the various outpatient departments. Past the corridor to the hospital canteen with the smell of overcooked cabbage. On and on past the physiotherapy department and the audiology department.

At the top of the stairs, I pass a large stained-glass window. Well, it's not so much a window, as it's got a wall behind it where they added on another building. They decided to keep it where it was, as it was made by Harry Clarke and they didn't want to risk moving it. It's quite a formidable piece: 'Visit of the Magi'. Lovely greens and blues and reds; someone had the bright idea to install some lights at the back. It depicts one of the wise men coming to visit Jesus the day he was born.

I go down the stairs and note the Child of Prague statue in a little alcove. It's quite anachronistic, seems like something that belongs to a different age when nuns and churches took care of the sick and dying. Obviously, this corner of the hospital was missed in the great secular sweep of the 1970s. The stairs open into a corridor, and you can see the pipes and plumbing that supplies the upper regions of the hospital. I almost get lost in the catacombs between Maintenance and Catering when I see a sign for the Department of Psychoanalysis. I follow it and find out this department is essentially just a library of dusty books with Lacan, Freud, and Jung on the covers.

I hurry through and pass the Department of Neuropsychiatry. I peep through the doors: 'ECT suite', 'EEG Room'. The subtle mix of terribly pragmatic and completely useless electronic gizmos; ECT machines for the shock therapy, EEG machines for brain wave recordings. I don't linger in case someone thinks I'm an escaping patient and follow the sign for Department of Liaison Psychiatry. Finally, I find myself outside the professor's office.

I knock – that sheepish *tap-tap* you make when you hope the person inside won't hear so you can report back to the boss that there was no one in the radiology department to discuss the CT brain scan with.

"Come in," said a male voice.

Just what I need: a psychiatrist with the ears of a fox.

"Hello. I'm, eh, Ciarán, I have a meeting with Professor King."

"Of course, welcome, welcome, come in."

A tall man, lanky, thin and grey as a ghost, bounces over to greet me. Mid-sixties. He has my hand in his, and it's one of those neuro-linguistic programming handshakes where he is trying to assert dominance and set boundaries. He finally releases me, and I shake my hand free, trying to break the line of hypnosis.

"Glass of water, Dr Murphy?"

Ah, that old chestnut, bribery masquerading as generosity. "Eh, no thanks."

He opens a door to the side and gestures for me to enter. Inside is, to be fair, a wonderful room. Textbook, even. Set up the exact way you'd set up a psychiatrist's office for a TV show. There are three or four diplomas in little pictures frames hanging on the far wall. A small but densely packed four-rowed bookcase to the side. Too many to skim, but I'm pretty sure I see a Harry Potter. A gigantic desk, banker's style dark wood, possibly mahogany, with one of those green and brass lamps. A phrenology skull with Fowler's name on it sits in one corner, an iMac in the centre, just behind that green fabric bit for writing on. The iMac is certainly not hospital issue. There are two comfortable-looking chairs in front of the desk, on the exit door side. And last but not least, what can only be described as a chaise longue in the far corner: a couch, leather, expensive-looking with one upturned end for the patient to lie back on.

"Take a seat, Dr Murphy." Professor King gestures to one of the comfy chairs. I sit down. It's a stark contrast to the chairs in the regular Department of Psychiatry. They're usually wooden or plastic, screwed to the floor to stop patients picking them up and chucking them, or cheeky doctors moving them into different offices.

"I thought you were going to ask me to lie down!" I smirk.

"Aha, the psychoanalysis couch." He nods towards the chaise longue. "More for show, really. From time to time, someone insists on it. Perhaps it makes them feel more comfortable with their role as a patient. I use it now for naps: a fifteen-minute siesta in the middle of the day does wonders for an old codger like me. Speaking of sleep, Dr Murphy, how has yours been these last few weeks?"

"Fine, actually…. Nice computer." I take another glance at the iMac on the desk. While sleek, it looks ancient.

"You can't beat the iMac G3. One of the last models that Steve Jobs actually had a hand in designing. I don't connect it to the internet or the hospital network at all – you can never be too careful with all those awful viruses out there."

There is a bit of an awkward silence. I am tempted to tell him about my own suspicions concerning the hospital IT system, but I hold back.

Professor King takes my medical history, and his process is surprisingly unremarkable. He is concise but comprehensive, gliding through my personal history: where I went to school, what my parents were like, the last time I was unwell. He's efficient, yet casual.

He summarises me to myself:

"So, you're a twenty-seven-year-old man, in your last week of intern year, no fixed plan for medical training next year. You've never been sick before, never been in hospital – certainly not since the day you were born. Had a cold or flu here and there, a chest infection, but no major medical illnesses. You have no family history of physical or mental illness, but there are, what you call, some 'neurotic' extended family members. No drugs, but plenty of alcohol. No voices, no delusions. Low mood and some anxiety, but situation-dependent and not pervasive. Up until

137

the…event last week, you've never had any sort of mental health problem…."

"Yes, that's more or less it. Is there a plan?"

"Have you ever heard of bibliotherapy, Dr Murphy?"

I don't like to admit when I don't know something, so I take an educated guess with a sprinkle of spoof. "Où est la bibliothèque?" I recall from French classes ten years ago. "Biblio…bible…book? Reading therapy? Book therapy?"

"That's correct. Excellent! Let's have a look at my bookcase."

I am delighted to have a chance to investigate his collection. I don't see an order. Does he arrange them by size? Genre? Alphabetically by author surname? I see Tolkien, I see CS Lewis, I see Pullman. Oxford fantasy? I see *Twilight* and *Fifty Shades of Grey*! Trashy Romance. I see Shakespeare, Dickens and Chaucer. All the classics. Jung's red book, Freud's Melancholia. Joseph Campbell. More psychoanalysis books. Stephen King, Agatha Christie. Plenty of Joyce. I pick up *Harry Potter and the Philosopher's Stone*. On the inside cover is written a note: *Thank you so much, Professor King. Best wishes, Jo.*

"Ah, perhaps not that one. A first edition, worth a pretty penny."

I return it to the shelf and stare into the abyss.

"Best not to take too long, just pluck what catches your imagination."

*HP Lovecraft: Essential Short Stories* catches my eye. I pick it out.

"An interesting choice. Are you familiar with the Cthulhu Mythos?"

This time, I don't think the bluff is necessary. "Not really, only what has leached into popular culture."

"Excellent. So, your treatment, which is your homework if you will, is for you to read this. Start anywhere you like, read for thirty minutes and then, without any planning, I want you to write. A stream of consciousness. Write as little or as much as you want. If your penmanship is typical of doctors these days, feel free to type it. Bring it back tomorrow, same time, same place."

Before I know it, I am ushered back into the corridor, and I am on my way. Retrace my steps. Grab a bite to eat, retire to the local Starbucks, read a bit of Lovecraft and type my first 'stream of consciousness'.

I return the next day, same time, same place. I present my work printed in a nice, neat Times New Roman font. I have to admit, there was a little inkling of validation-seeking. There was, at the back of my mind, a desire to get a little pat on the head.

"Do you mind if I read aloud, Dr Murphy?" the professor asked.

I suppose the time for bashfulness was long gone. "Go right ahead!" I said.

Professor King, I admit, was a bit of a showman.

He had one of those voices suited for lecturing or, perhaps, moonlighting as an audio book narrator. He began.

"Last night, I was working in the hospital. It was Easter Sunday. The doctors were gone, as were the nurses, the cleaners and other denizens of the wards. Of course, the poor creatures in the beds and trolleys were there, chained allegorically by their illnesses.

"I completed my rounds on the wards, carrying pills and loaded syringes. Dressed in my white-coat armour, I had a utility belt of instruments, a reflex hammer, a pen torch, a stethoscope, a funduscope, a sphygmometer, and a thermometer. Feeble weapons in my arsenal against the severely morbid."

Professor King paused.

"Interesting, a story about a novice doctor? A medical student even?"

"Yes."

He continued.

"The hospital had fallen into disarray. The floors were tacky, each step leaving a trace in the slime that draped the tiles. The walls were alive with lichenous grime, the metallic fixtures now a venomous green. A fetid darkness engulfed each room. From each bed, a gangrenous glare or chlorotic stare met me. Neither pleading nor defiant, their countenance empty now of all discernible emotion. Putrescent juices seeped out of leprous wounds."

Another pause. "I see the Lovecraftian influence

is strong. Quite visceral here, florid even."

I blushed. It was a little nerve-wracking to have the story dissected paragraph by paragraph. I suddenly felt a rush of anxiety sweep over me. What was I revealing about myself through this story? He continued.

"The hospital building was a labyrinth. There were no signposts or directions. Each stair brought me down into another grotto where I would carry out further impotent tasks."

"A Labyrinth? Like the one in Crete, created by Daedalus, reminiscent of Joyce's…."

"Stephen Dedalus." I chimed in.

"Exactly. Let's continue."

"In previous days, the religious relics – hearts of saints, fingers of priests, the cloak of Saint Patrick, stood proud at the end of each room, holy roods graced the walls. Iconographic paintings and plaques had filled the corridors, but now they were simply catacombs of a nameless menace."

"Oh my. This might take a re-reading. There's a lot going on here. A lament for more religious times? Or perhaps, a lament for when we could name and identify the powers that pulled the strings?"

"I actually hadn't really thought of that. I was just commenting on how some places have religious bits and pieces around and some…don't," I said.

He continued.

"I earnestly made my way lower and lower into

the subterraneous belly of this beast. In the perpetual darkness, my orb of self-righteousness was my light. I was here to do the good work of the Lord, to cure the sick and free the possessed."

"It is a labyrinth, I see. The normal rules of physics don't apply. Perhaps then, this is a dream world?" the professor probed.

"Well, funnily enough, it is a little bit based on a reoccurring dream I had." I was thrown off by my own honesty.

"I finally came to a locked door, with a grotesque gargoyle standing sentry. Behind the door, I heard the uncontrolled laugher and shrieking of pure madness. Curiosity and duty overwhelmed the sense of fear stemming from my amygdala as my dorsolateral prefrontal cortex shot warning signs at it."

"Amygdala? Prefrontal cortex? You can take the doctor out of anatomy lessons, but you can't take the anatomy lessons out of the doctor!" the professor quipped and quickly continued.

"I took from my belt my swipe card and inserted it into a gargoyle's mouth. It transformed into a huge skeleton key. The great gothic cast iron door swung open and beckoned me into a sinister room. Although the room was dark, a lurid greenish hue illuminated parts, like the effect of night goggles."

"Aha, the lanyard proletariat to the rescue. The setting is jumbled here. It's like a modern hospital combined with a medieval cathedral. What's the commentary? Despite the electronics and the gadgets, modern medicine is nothing more efficacious than modern soothsaying and bloodletting?" The professor looked right at me.

When it was opened up like that, it all sounded a bit on the nose. Grandiose and silly. The ramblings of a naïve fool. My silence prompted him to continue.

"As I entered into the abysm, my white coat was replaced by a golden robe, my utility belt a leather satchel. My medical instruments now a short sword, a strong buckler, a vial of holy water and a Bible. Inside, I found the consultants. Some were concocting vile potions in cauldrons, others were creating instruments of torture…but most were sitting around feasting and counting their gold coins."

"Ah, the lazy powermongers, like Roman senators.

"They were in a different form: demonesque, gross, terrible. Some had many limbs, like an octopus. Others crawled the walls like spiders with human heads, whilst others still flew like winged beetles, their elytra iridescent."

"Yes, quite Lovecraftian here. He was a terrible racist, you know." The professor said with a smile twitching at the corners of his mouth.

"Yes, well, I read an article critiquing this. Some say we should cut him from the syllabus." I said, noncommittally.

"Indeed, some say a lot of things these days," the professor answered.

"As I moved further and further into the depths of this, my uncertainty left me, and I rose from the stupor like a Crusader. I discarded my pyrite robe. I opened the Bible and took out the holy waters. Then I began to chant:

*Exorcizamus te, omnis immundus spiritus*
*omnis satanica potestas, omnis incursio*
*infernalis adversarii, omnis legio,*
*omnis congregatio et secta diabolica."*

"The Exorcist! Fantastic film. Pyrite is, if I can recall, fool's gold, is it? And an armed priest…?"

"A paladin," I supplied.

"A paladin, of course, riding on Rocinante? A little more Arthurian than Lovecraftian in this section."

I said nothing.

"When they heard this, the consultant demons gave out a ululant wail and turned their attention towards me. They swooped and swarmed me, but my Bible and crucifix held them off. I swiped at them with holy waters and scalded their scaly skin.

"I chased them out, and those I caught, I drenched. I pressed my crucifix to their bodies and branded them with the sign of the cross. I placed the Bible on their heads and compelled the demons to leave. In a hiss of smoke and toxic gas, the image of the demon would melt away into sticky protoplasm, leaving a naked, helpless consultant curled in a ball."

"Now *this* reminds me of one of those action

movies. The one with the vampire hunter."

"*Blade*?" I proposed.

"Yes indeed," he chuckled.

"After minutes – or maybe it was hours – my work was done. I had expelled the darkness. The green light faded to a more benign yellow glow of fluorescent tubes. The cauldrons of overpriced potions which I had knocked over were revealed to be overpriced medications. The torturous equipment faded away and left MRI scanners. The private rooms in the bowels of the hospital converted back to public outpatient clinics. The Gargoyle phased back into the key card reader."

"That's it?"

"Well, that's where the dream ends."

"Not much of ending, is it? Feels a little unfinished. Well, let's see. What did we learn?"

"It's just a dream," I shrugged.

"Indeed, a cigar is sometimes just a cigar."

"Did Freud ever actually say that?"

"No, I don't think so. What shall we call it, then? An acute stress reaction? Someone working a little too much without enough rest and recovery? Too much stress and a brief period of being overwhelmed."

"That sounds about right," I conceded.

"We must, of course, monitor for mental illness. There is a chance it was the first episode of Bipolar Affective Disorder, or indeed, perhaps, a Schizophreniform illness." He said this last bit gently.

"Schizophrenia?" I whispered.

"There's a chance, albeit small. That's why we must keep an eye on you. For next week, what will you read?"

I returned to the bookcase. The selection was different, I swear. I couldn't see *Harry Potter*.

Kafka, Doskokreveksy, Tolsoy, Cervantes. Dumas, Twain. I closed my eyes and reached out. "*The Metamorphosis*," I said.

"*The Metamorphosis*." he echoed.

# The Institute of Immortality Studies

Henry O'Connell

*We embrace our children to be folded in the arms of the future,*
*to pass ourselves on beyond death, to be transported.*
— **Age of Iron, J. M. Coetzee**

Professor Rory O'Brien opened his eyes just before the alarm clock went off, as always. This was one of his favourite parts of the day, when he felt like he was the first person in the world to wake up.

He looked at Marie, his still-sleeping wife, and smiled, leaning over to gently kiss a bare shoulder. He got up slowly and silently from the bed, feeling a mild ache in his knees and back, and stepped into his slippers. When he showered and shaved, it was in an automatic fashion. He found that his body was reluctant to shake the comfort of sleep; his dreams were almost tangible as he went through the motions of his morning ritual, floating over and back in a Yeatsian fog between the dark of night and the half-light of the early summer morning. Last night, his dreams were all about his daughter Chloe, who had often watched him shaving in this bathroom decades before, asking him endless questions while he tried to escape from the house to get to his Institute. When he was dressed, he descended the stairs to the kitchen, made some tea and buttered toast for his wife, and then took a breakfast tray back upstairs, where he placed it gently on her bedside table.

"Rise and shine, sleepy head," he whispered.

She sat up and yawned. "Darling, be careful on the bike. I hope you make a big breakthrough today!" she called after him as he hurried back down the stairs.

He smiled to himself at this: one of their long-running jokes about his work.

"And don't forget about our visitor tonight. Don't be late!"

As if he *could* forget. He had thought of nothing else since the phone call. Chloe was now in her thirties and had grown into a beautiful, bright young woman – just like her mother. She had established herself at a national newspaper as a highly respected journalist quickly after university until she had transitioned to freelancing as a writer in London. She was completely dedicated to her work, just like he had been at her age, so O'Brien and his wife were all the more surprised and thrilled when she had rung two weeks earlier to say that she would be breaking the habit of a lifetime to take a holiday, which she would spend at home with them in Dublin.

O'Brien packed his backpack with the essentials for the day, carefully fitted his helmet and wheeled his bicycle out of the porch and onto the front driveway. It was fully bright now, and the early summer day was already starting to feel warm. He mounted the bike and slowly eased onto Cedar Drive. He then took a right onto Wellington Drive and lazily cycled the two miles to Hibernian College. There were only a few cars on the road – the same ones he always met at this time. As he cycled, he tried to calculate how many hours he must have spent plotting his career on this journey through the years, always cycling away from his wife and their little girl to get to the peace and solitude of his once-famous Institute.

He arrived at Hibernian College, dismounted, and locked his bicycle. The small college campus was silent apart from a few foraging crows and pigeons at the bins. He walked across the 'quad', as he and his Hibernian College colleagues liked to call it, with self-deprecating humour. It was a far cry from the quads of Trinity College Dublin or other great universities. His Institute was in the 'Boyle Block'. This building had begun as an afterthought in the history of the college; Hibernian College was already ten years old when The Robert Boyle Science Academy was built in 1975.

O'Brien's fascination with ageing had started when he was a doctor. He had specialised in Old Age Psychiatry, treating people with dementia and other age-related conditions, but grew frustrated with the lack of any sign of curative treatments on the research horizon after just a few short years. So, with youthful ambition, he had left clinical medicine and embarked on his own research career, focussing on the many mysteries and challenges of ageing.

He typed in the security code and took the elevator to the basement. The automatic door opened, and there, in front of him, facing him for perhaps the five thousandth time, was the door of his own Institute. The sign was now fifteen years old and mocked him more and more each year.

*Institute of Immortality Studies. Head of Department: Prof. R. O'Brien*

Even when he had commissioned the sign – a time when he was at the height of his powers and ambitions – the title of the Institute had jarred with him slightly. He had thought of it after a plane journey where the passenger next to him had been somewhat disparaging of his work, which was based at the time on starving rats and seeing how it affected their health and longevity.

"How the hell is that important?" the passenger had asked.

He had fantasised before the plane touched down about his then-fledgling Institute and his quest for anti-ageing therapies and wondered what a truly remarkable and self-explanatory title for such an Institute would be, hence: The Institute of Immortality Studies. In the early years, he had ignored any slight embarrassments caused by the sign, hoping that such a title would inspire everyone who walked through its doors, a bit like the way the 'This is Anfield' sign of his beloved Liverpool Football Club is meant to inspire the club's players and intimidate its opponents.

The Institute was tiny, consisting of only three rooms. One room served as a reception, where a secretary used to sit before they ran out of funding. The room to the left had once belonged to the eager students that scurried around the Institute, and the room to the right of the reception room was his office. But those rooms had been empty for quite some time. O'Brien had been the sole occupant of the Institute now for the past five years.

He turned on his computer and checked his emails. There was a blanket email from Mike Cooper in the California Centre for Biological Sciences:

To all my Irish buddies. I will be visiting the west of Ireland between July 15th and August 3rd this year. Call my cell-phone (see number below) to meet for a pint of Guinness.

*"So that's what's come of my relationship with the great Professor Cooper,"* O'Brien thought wistfully.

He often reminisced about the three seminal

papers on caloric restriction and delayed ageing in rats that they had produced together in the early 1990s. He remembered how Cooper had been charmingly incredulous that O'Brien had produced such impressive work on a shoestring budget, having a research grant of only twenty thousand pounds and the aid of two part-time postgraduate students who were happy to work practically for free. Cooper had produced similar results at the same time as O'Brien. The difference had been that he'd had the backing of two million dollars and a team of five other top researchers. When Cooper received a humble letter from O'Brien describing his preliminary results, he'd had him flown to California, where he showed him around his laboratory and offered him a research position in the sunshine. Cooper had said that the two of them were a lot like Charles Darwin and Alfred Russel Wallace, discovering their great theory at the same time. The implication, of course, had been that O'Brien was the part of the young and humble Wallace and Cooper the older, wealthier and more established Darwin.

They co-authored the three papers and became quite famous as a result – at least in the world of anti-ageing scientists. That was as good as it got for O'Brien. He loved the interviews with mainstream newspapers and radio stations, always introduced as a 'leading expert'. He sometimes worried that he loved the media exposure more than the tedium of slaughtering rats, slicing them up and looking at their brains under a microscope. There were times during those few years when O'Brien couldn't sleep for excitement, and he would jump out of bed every morning with an urgency to get to the Institute and get ahead of his research rivals. But things had changed. Cooper had moved on to add a few more minor findings on his own. O'Brien had not taken up the offer to work in California because of his daughter's schooling in Dublin, and he had achieved hardly anything more. Now, the great Cooper was sending out block emails looking for a drinking buddy.

At 9 a.m., O'Brien made some instant coffee and started to look at his current research proposals. There were five in total, all relating to different aspects of ageing. Unfortunately, all of them had been written and revised several times over the past few years, and they had all been rejected for funding on multiple occasions by the Irish National Research Foundation and other such bodies. He added some references and corrected some grammatical errors, but he knew in his heart that the proposals were stale and no longer of any interest to the scientific establishment. He blushed a little as he thought about the wording of a recent rejection letter for a grant application.

Professor O'Brien has an established track record in the area of ageing and, specifically, caloric restriction. However, his proposal is overly ambitious for the funds that are available from the Irish National

Research Foundation. In any event, the proposal is not in itself novel, considering the work that has been carried out in The Cooper Institute in California.

*"The Cooper Institute,"* thought O'Brien. *"I hope he doesn't decide to visit me on his trip here."*

He remembered Cooper's last trip a few years before. In an effort to impress, he had to pretend that the whole Boyle Block was the Institute of Immortality Studies. He had joked with Marie at the time that in pretending the whole Boyle Block was his research realm that he felt like Puss in Boots trying to impress the king, a favourite bedtime story of Chloe's at the time. And Cooper, with his American scale on everything, was not even impressed with that. But he didn't envy or dislike Cooper. Cooper was doing what O'Brien could have done if he'd had the funding. There was no magic to Cooper's work. He was simply churning out results to confirm hypotheses that he and O'Brien had proposed two decades before.

O'Brien then checked his online lecturing timetable at 10 a.m. and saw that, due to cancellations, he had no lectures to give today. He heaved a sigh of relief. Even though the fourteen hours of lectures he gave every week were now his main source of income, he dreaded them. They were so far from what he wanted to be doing – or at least, so far from what he *thought* he should be doing.

So, with the rest of the day effectively free, O'Brien leaned back in his chair and started flicking idly through the pages of his current copy of *The Ageing Cell*, thinking of Chloe, who would be back in their house tonight for the first time in so long. He daydreamed as he read. There was a new article on so-called zombie cells and how they may be central to the ageing process. They accumulated with age and then 'infected' neighbouring young and healthy cells with a tendency to age and die, thus setting up a domino ageing effect and a cascade towards death.

The zombie cell phenomenon was the effect that being with some of his older friends had on O'Brien; they made him feel older than he was, with their ailments and regrets. He sometimes longed to have young assistants and associates working with him again in the Institute, to help stave off the spread of zombie cells in his own mind and spirit.

Then he brought his thoughts back to his research with Cooper and wondered how caloric restriction could be used to starve out these beastly zombie cells. And then he wondered how many hours he must have wasted in this office over the years while Marie and Chloe waited for him at home. He was still sitting in the same office, waiting for Chloe to arrive in a place where he wasn't. He started to nod off into a light sleep, a habit he had developed in recent years.

Half an hour later, he jumped at the shrill ring from the telephone on his desk, a telephone that was largely silent in recent years. It was Marie.

"She's early. She'll be here in ten minutes. Come

home and be careful on that bike."

He didn't give himself time to answer, but sprang into action immediately. He threw down the receiver and locked up the Institute, thumbing madly at the elevator call button. As soon as the doors pinged open, he ran across the quad, jumped on his bike, and started cycling frantically. He didn't even stop to think that he had left his backpack and helmet on his desk.

The roads were thick with mid-day traffic, and he felt like the journey home was taking an age. His heart began to race as the front wheel of his bicycle finally rolled onto Wellington Drive. She would be nearly there by now, kissing and hugging Marie.

He turned the corner onto Cedar Drive. There was his house, and there was a taxi parked outside. He strained his eyes to make out three figures. The driver was handing bags from the boot to Marie and Chloe.

O'Brien could hold back no longer. "Chloe!" he called out, breathless as he cycled faster towards them.

She turned to look at him, and her face lit up instantly with a warm and familiar smile.

# DEAR MR SHANKLY

Henry O'Connell

Email
From: patbyrne1959@yahoo.com
To: mike@footieclips.com
Subject: YouTube clip of Bill Shankly's retirement
Sent: 05/09/2020 at 08.13

Dear Mike,

I've watched your recent YouTube clip about a hundred times over the past week – the one about the retirement of Bill Shankly – and I just wanted to let you know some background information that you might find interesting. (I didn't want to post this on the public comments below your video, as it's a very private story, but I thought I would share with you directly my own memories about the day in question, in confidence.)

Apparently, Andy Warhol said in 1968 that, 'in the future, everyone will be world-famous for fifteen minutes.' I'm not sure exactly what he was getting at, and I never gave the saying much thought, but then I discovered last week with your video that I actually *did* have my own brief episode of fame many years ago, and I didn't even realise it at the time. It wasn't quite the fifteen minutes that Warhol talked about; more like fifteen seconds. But I was famous all right – briefly anyway – because I got on the telly. And I didn't even know it until I saw your clip on YouTube last week, shown to me by my granddaughter.

As you know, the date of the original video was 12th July, 1974, and a reporter was roaming the streets of Liverpool asking random people what they thought about the sudden retirement of Bill Shankly earlier that day. As Shankly was the saviour and he remains (in my opinion) the greatest ever manager of Liverpool Football Club, the news of his retirement sent shock waves throughout the city, among footballing and non-footballing people alike. Everyone in the video is shaken and sad – apart from the occasional Everton fan, who smiles and jokes, seeing it is a potential reprieve from the domination of red over blue in their city.

And then, in the middle of all the interviews, there's a teenage boy with long fair hair who seems to be taking the news worse than most.

"What do you think of Bill Shankly retiring?" asks the reporter, shoving the microphone in the boy's face.

"Don't believe you," the boy says, squaring up to

the reporter. For a second, it looks like going to thump the reporter. And then, when the reporter calmly reiterates the news, the boy stands back and becomes a bit more thoughtful. "Mr Shankly would never do that," he says. "Mr Shankly maybe just needs to take a holiday." Then the initial anger turns to near-tears when, with a quiver in his voice, he says, "Mr Shankly has too much work to do. We haven't won the European Cup yet." And then the reporter moves on to his next random passer-by.

The boy, of course, was me.

And looking at the YouTube clip again and again over the past week, there's no doubt that it was me. I'm wearing that red jumper of mine, with a white shirt inside – my effort at sporting the Liverpool colours back in a time when replica jerseys were a yet-to-be-dreamed-of luxury. And that was my hair, all right. It was straight and fair and long, with a fringe, like my hero Steve Heighway, an Irishman who played as a winger with Shankly's great team. And I know that I was fourteen going on fifteen at the time, because I was born in 1959, the year that Bill Shankly signed as Liverpool manager.

But I really don't remember the interview being done. Maybe I didn't notice the camera and the microphone, hard as that might be to believe. Maybe I was too shocked at the news to realise that I was being interviewed. Or, maybe it was because of the other stuff that was going on at the time, especially that morning. You see, now we're getting to that background information I promised you.

My mum was a drinker. In fact, she was an alcoholic, and a bad one at that. Things had been getting worse and worse with her in 1974, with 12th July being the day it got *really* bad.

12th July was a funny kind of day in Liverpool. Liverpool was, and remains, a very Irish city. And because of all the Irish in the city, there was a fair bit of Catholic-Protestant needle there up until the 1970s at least; a minor version of what was happening back in Ireland itself. There were even a few small Orangeman's parades in Liverpool in the lead up to the 12th to mark the Battle of the Boyne. It's all a bit crazy now when you think of it: Irish immigrants marching in the streets of an English city to commemorate a battle that occurred three centuries before in Ireland, between a Dutch king and an English king, while other Irish immigrants look on in disgust!

The Irish orange-green divide had some convoluted link too to the red-blue football divide of the city. Everton fans liked to say that *they* were the 'true' Liverpool club and that Liverpool Football Club was only for immigrants and blow-ins. But Irish-Catholic Everton fans liked to say that Everton was the team for Irish Catholics and Liverpool FC was for Protestants and the English. My parents both had Irish and Catholic roots, so maybe I should have supported Everton. But the kids on our street – all with Irish names like mine – paid no heed to these mangled history lessons. They just followed who they liked, resulting in a fairly even red-blue divide. It was because Bill Shankly arrived in Liverpool at the same time I was born into the world that I chose the red team.

Anyway. Where was I? Ah yes – 12th July, 1974 was a Friday, and I remember my mum had been out drinking the night before. She was in the middle of a two-week-long binge. Dad was working in the factory, doing a night shift. My brother had just moved to London. So, I was on my own in the house that night, hoping she wouldn't be too late or too drunk. To help the time pass and to get my mind off worrying about her, I was 'doing my Liverpool stuff.'

'Doing my Liverpool stuff' was my mum's phrase. She knew very little about football, but she mostly admired my little hobby, knowing that it kept me quiet and off the streets at night. And it was cheaper than collecting stamps or making model aeroplanes. My 'Liverpool stuff' was a huge collection of scrapbooks and ordinary school copybooks, each one full of newspaper clippings and facts and figures relating to my club. I had started it when I was nine, and now, five years later, it took up one whole half of the bedroom I had – until recently – shared with my brother.

In the copybooks, I would record details of every single game on the night of that game or, at the very latest, the following day. In the early years, I would get my information from late-night radio broadcasts or simply word-of-mouth from older lads who had been at the game. I can still remember tuning in to the late sports results at ten or eleven at night, hanging on every word of the broadcaster as he went down through the list of results, my heart stopping as he said the word 'Liverpool' and then gave the score.

But I grew up less than a mile from Anfield, and, as I got older, I would sneak into the stadium to watch matches with a few of my friends. The men at the gates used to wave us through and into the schoolboy section; sometimes, we even managed to climb over the fence from the schoolboy enclosure and get into The Kop itself. Being in The Kop was like being at war, surrounded by roaring comrades, all with the same purpose in mind, with everyone full of singing swagger but also secretly terrified of defeat. I was smaller than everyone around me, trying my best not to be trampled or peed on by the bigger boys and men.

My 'Liverpool stuff' got a lot more detailed once I was able to get into Anfield. I would have, as a minimum, the basics of the opposition, score, venue and scorers all recorded in a copybook. This was a time when football squads were less than half the size of modern squads, and only one sub was allowed. So the starting team was almost always the same – no such thing as squad rotation back then. For each game, I would also have some observations of my own, and these observations got more detailed as the years went by, with comments on things like individual players, or how the opposition lined up against us, or gaps in the team that could only be filled by a new signing.

The bigger scrapbooks had cut-outs of match reports and photographs of all the players from the newspapers. There were the stars of the first half of the 1960s like Ron Yeats, Ian St. John and Roger Hunt. Hunt was a scoring machine, and he had dragged Liverpool out of the Second Division, under the leadership of Bill Shankly. Then Shankly had brought in superstars like Yeats and St. John; the team had gone on to win the First Division twice and, for the first time in the history of the club, the FA Cup. I was only five when they won that FA Cup, but I have vague memories of the homecoming, the streets lined with thousands, red and white everywhere.

By the time I started my 'Liverpool stuff', the 1960s team was in decline, even though I didn't know it at the time. Shankly sold off the stars of the 1960s and then brought in new heroes for the new decade, heroes who would go on to take Liverpool to more trophies. The first big signing of the new decade was the Irish man Steve Heighway, on whom I based my hairstyle. I remember his searing runs up and down the wings, always skipping past the brutish tackles. Then there was big John Toshack and his partner in crime, little Kevin Keegan. And there was Peter

Cormack and Jimmy Case. Liverpool would win the league again in 1973 along with the UEFA Cup, our first big European trophy. Then came another FA Cup in 1974, with Liverpool hammering Newcastle United 3-0 in the final. Apparently, some Liverpool supporters who got onto the Wembley pitch after that final bowed at Shankly's feet. They didn't know that it would be his last game in charge of the club and that two months later, he would be announcing his retirement.

As my knowledge of the game grew, I started to write letters directly to Bill Shankly himself. These were always written in the most respectful and reserved of styles, but with subtle hints as to how he might improve things. The letters always began with 'Dear Mr Shankly'. A week or so after sending the letter, I would get an acknowledgement slip back from Anfield, but never an actual letter from the great man himself. My mother would hand me the letters when they arrived, looking on hopefully as I opened them, knowing how much I wished the next one might be from 'Shanks', as she always called him.

There were a dozen boys on our street my age, and we were all football mad. We had our own little alleyway where we played crazy matches of four, five or six aside. The matches would go on all evening until the streets were dark and the faint light of the streetlamp was no longer enough for us to be able to see the ball. The final scores in those games might be

19-17 or crazy scores like that. We knew it was getting too dark when, as the football fizzed around, it started to develop a kind of tail chasing it, as if it were a comet.

Boys who couldn't sit still for five minutes in a classroom earlier in the day never lost count of the score in those epic games. Even now, whenever I get a whiff of chimney smoke on a winter's evening, I am almost immediately back there to that alleyway and those frantic, endless games.

I was a solid-enough player myself, but I had none of the skills of fellas like Paddy Dempsey or Anthony Ryan from our street. And I wasn't as big or strong as lads like Matt Walsh or Micky Brennan. But I always seemed to end up on the winning team, because I seemed to have a knack for tactics and setting the team up right. I would usually play in midfield or on the right wing, driving the team forward, but always first to drop back if we came under pressure. I couldn't do the solo runs or tricks or long shots of the others, but I had an instinct for being in the right place at the right time and nicking the ball off someone's toe or getting on the end of a cross to finish off a move. Of course, I liked to think that made me like Bill Shankly himself – a solid player who never really shone but would go on to become the greatest manager and leader that Liverpool Football Club ever had.

And straight after those alleyway games, it was in for tea and then upstairs to do my homework and then my 'Liverpool stuff'. The truth is that my 'Liverpool stuff' and my letters to Bill Shankly were a good distraction from what was going on in our house at the time too. While my mum liked me doing my 'Liverpool stuff' because it kept me off the streets at night, I liked doing it because it kept my mind off her when she was on one of her benders.

You see, Mum could go through months of not touching alcohol. Those times were happy and normal. The colour would come back in her cheeks, and she would be perfect in every way. She would have dinner for us every evening, and she would be full of hugs and kisses. She even had a little job down at the corner shop, and she would get back into it. Everyone on the road loved her; when she was off the drink, the light came back inside her, like she was a girl again.

But then she would have a 'slip'. The term sounds so harmless. But the 'slips' were bloody awful. It would start with her going for 'a small one' after work and then a few more the next evening. Then the 'slip' would turn into a 'bender' that might last a week, often two. During a 'bender', she could come home at any time of the day or night. I used to get cross (in my head only, of course) with my dad, as he would just keep going to work at the factory as if everything was normal. I realise now that he had been dealing with her slips and benders for years, and he had given up trying to turn the tide.

During the sober times, she would sometimes come up to my room with a copy of 'Roy of the Rovers' or some other football comic. She would leave it on my bed and smile at me. I think it was her way of asking for forgiveness. I'm starting to realise now that she could do little about the benders, especially as the years went on.

Lots of other lads on the street knew about 'slips' and 'benders', as lots of the Dads were drinkers. But having your mum an alcoholic was unusual – and a lot worse in some ways. The women were supposed to be at home keeping things together, cooking and washing and darning and nagging their kids to do their homework. And my mum would be like that when she was sober. But things got messy when she went on the benders. You might find her lying face-down on the floor of the toilet or slumped on the sofa, covered in vomit. I'm sorry to have to say those things, but they're the truth of the matter.

When I was twelve or thirteen, I started to become aware that the men around had a view of her, that they looked at her differently to the other mothers. One day in school, a boy told me that my mum 'would do anything you like for a glass of whiskey', and I bashed his head against a wall until he passed out.

The morning of 12th July, 1974, was when things got really bad, as if they hadn't been bad enough over the previous years. I know now that my brother had moved to London because he couldn't stand living in the same house as my mother anymore. And my father was taking on any extra shifts going so he could get away from her, too. I got up late that Friday morning, as it was school holidays and I had the day to myself. I had a look at my 'Liverpool stuff' and finished off a letter to Bill Shankly, suggesting that maybe Liverpool needed to start playing Kevin Keegan in a deeper role, along with some training suggestions for the close season. I skipped down the stairs with the envelope in my hand, off to catch the morning post. I hadn't heard Mum coming in the night before, and I assumed she was sleeping off her drink.

Then I found her at the bottom of the stairs. Her face was caked in blood, and she was slumped across the last three steps, her head on the floor. Dad was working.

When the ambulance pulled away with her, I started to realise how my dad and my brother must have felt, living in that house with her, being responsible for her, for the first time. She might make it back home, or she might not. If she made it home, she would slip again in a few weeks – or sooner, as the slips seemed to be getting more frequent. The way she looked that morning made me realise that she could only have so many more of these slips.

I dried my tears and punched the hall door a few times and picked my letter to Mr Shankly from off the floor. Shankly had escaped a life in the coal mines in Scotland to become a professional football player. He had fought the Germans in World War II. He had dragged Liverpool out of the Second Division and led us to three First Division titles, two FA Cups and a UEFA Cup. He was the one who decided that Liverpool would wear all red, to show opposition teams how strong and dangerous we were. He was the one who turned Anfield into – in his own words – a 'bastion of invincibility'. He knew how tough life was, but he always remained hopeful, and he never stopped fighting. Everything he did was for the fans of Liverpool Football Club.

I remember catching glimpses of him from The Kop at moments when games were going against Liverpool. He would stick out his chest and chin and move his arms around with purpose, directing and encouraging and willing the team on.

I used to act like Shankly during those matches of ours in the alleyway, especially if my team was losing. I would look at our own little version of Anfield and size up the two teams, and then, like magic, a solution would come into my head. I might tell John Sullivan to drop back for a few minutes, or I might go in goal myself and leave all the best players outfield. And the changes I made usually worked. After that, I would go home and head upstairs and, after skipping through the dull homework as fast as possible, take out my 'Liverpool stuff' and think about the next big game and how Shankly was going to deliver another victory for the reds. So football in the alleyway and in my bedroom kept my mind off my mother's descent into hell.

So as the ambulance pulled away and I licked my knuckles, bloodied from punching the front door, I stopped crying. I stopped worrying about my mother and decided that the most important thing I needed to do that Friday morning was to post my letter to Mr Shankly and then get home to organise (for the thousandth time) my 'Liverpool stuff'. I knew that I could lose myself for a few hours by sorting through the copybooks and scrapbooks and planning out the first games of the new 1974-1975 season, just a few weeks ahead.

It must have been on my trip home from the Post Office, having just posted my letter to Bill Shankly, that the reporter stopped me and told me the news of the retirement.

This explains the look I have of wanting to thump him at first. The quiver in my voice is harder to explain: it was because of a few things, I think. First and foremost, it was because Shankly had abandoned us. But it was also because I had a funny feeling that I might not see my mum again. And now that Shankly had gone and left us, I wouldn't have the comfort of my 'Liverpool stuff' to keep my mind off Mum. How could I keep on making my childish notes and writing those stupid letters when they clearly had no impact on anyone? Shankly didn't even have the manners to reply to me once.

As I say, I don't remember the interview. But I do remember getting home and taking all my 'Liverpool stuff' and piling it into a cardboard box, which I left in the shed out the back. No more childish things for me. No more scrapbooks and foolish fandom. Bill Shankly and my mum had seen to that.

She was in hospital for a few weeks after that and then went to stay in some type of hostel. My brother came home for a while to keep an eye on Dad and me. I remember he was awkward and trying to act the part of a man, even though he was still just a boy himself. We never mentioned Mum.

Then a woman came to the house to take Mum's things to her. She left with two suitcases and a few parcels and envelopes. She told us that Mum would be staying at the hostel for a while and that she would be home to us after that. I didn't believe her.

The inevitable happened, of course. Mum sneaked out of the hostel late one night and went on a week-long bender. Her body was found in a park beside the hostel. The coroner ruled out foul play, at least.

Six months after Mum died, a solicitor came to the house with a briefcase and a look of professional pity. My dad asked me to wait in my bedroom as he dealt with everything quickly at the kitchen table, signing a few documents and thanking the solicitor.

When the solicitor left, I was called down to the kitchen, and Dad gave me an envelope, which I took back to my room. On the outside was Mum's writing, with a date of 5th July, 1974.

*Dear Pat, this just arrived from Anfield. It might be one of the usual 'thank you' letters from the club, or this time it might actually be from Shanks himself! I haven't opened it. Good luck, and here's hoping. Love, Mum.*

I opened the envelope and noted the usual Liverpool Football Club headed notepaper. But instead of the usual official and impersonal note from the club, this time it was an actual letter, and it was from the man himself!

I have copied the letter below, as I thought you might like to read it.

*With all my best wishes,*
*Pat Byrne*

Liverpool Football Club and Athletic Grounds Co. Ltd.
Anfield Road
Liverpool
L4 0TH

5th July, 1974
Anfield

*Dear Pat,*

*I have counted up your letters to me, and they now come to one hundred! Managing Liverpool Football Club is such a busy job that I rarely get time to answer letters. But when a lad sends me a hundred letters, I have to reply!*

*I always think of your advice about the different players and your suggestions about who we should be buying for the season ahead. I also try to take your advice on young players in the city and send scouts to matches as you suggest, when possible.*

*You are right to be so honest about your own abilities. It sounds like you will be a great manager and coach. But don't give up on playing either, as you will only be able to play for so many years, and before you know it, you will be too old. Even if you don't have the same skill as some of the others, just work hard at always being fit and fighting hard in every game – that is more than half the battle won.*

*I'm very sorry to hear that your dear mother has been so sick and I wish her well, along with your brother in London and your hard-working dad.*
*As for myself, I have achieved a lot with this great club, but I have neglected my own family for too long. I have grown tired, and I know that I must now make a big change. You will learn about the change soon, and I hope that you are not too disappointed.*

*I wish you every success for the future. Remember, no matter what life throws at you, you must always be prepared for the worst and fight like your life depends on it. Once you accept that, then you will never be afraid, and life will be easier.*

*And for as long as you are a supporter of this great club – which will be forever – remember our anthem, and you will truly never walk alone.*

*With all my best wishes,*
*Bill Shankly*

# THE SICKNESS

Kevin Lally

A woman busied herself in her kitchen. She added wood to the stove – not so much to make it smoke, but enough to get up the heat – and bent over a basin of water that she had carted up from the well earlier that day. She added kindling in groups of two or three, never more, never less. She dipped her ladle into the basin and swirled it twice clockwise and three times anticlockwise, then poured the water into a large copper pot. It splashed, but there was no steam, which told her it wasn't hot enough yet. She cursed. She would have to start the ritual again.

She was making mistakes now that she hadn't made for years. Her intrusive thoughts were returning, worse than ever. Should she tell her husband the truth? She wasn't sure how much longer she could continue living this lie.

Though her back was turned to the wooden porch, she still heard the soft footfalls of a horse and the sound of a wagon being drawn through the mud and tensed. A man approached. He wore a fedora hat, which was the norm, but also a kerchief covering his face, outlaw style. Like something from the old cowboy movies her grandfather used to show her. As the man moved into focus, she recognised the kerchief as one she had boiled the day before in carbolic soap. She exhaled, though she hadn't realised she was holding her breath.

Carol added more wood to the stove. It smoked. She took a knife from the table and scraped some soap into the water. It started to bubble. She took a sprig of lavender from the windowsill and added that into the water, too. Before long, it bubbled, and steam rose into the air. *What I wouldn't give for some store-bought detergent. Alcohol hand sanitiser.* Is this the time to tell him the secret she had been hiding since the day they met?

"You're back early." She moved away from the stove and leant against the doorframe, her arms folded across her chest.

The man pulled the kerchief down from his face. It looked as though he hadn't shaved in a day or two, and his skin was tanned like leather. There was a shade of fear in his eyes. "There's no business in town anymore. Either everyone is taken to their beds, or they're afraid to leave their houses in case they get the sickness." The man moved to enter.

"Wait. Stay outside. I'll bring the water to you."

"Now, wait a second," he growled. "This is still my house. No one tells me when I can and can't come in."

"Please," she placated. She heaved the hot pot of water off the stove. She put it out on the porch. She didn't spill a drop. "Please, wash up now. Up to the elbows like I showed you."

"What about behind my ears as well?"

"I don't mean to be mothering you, Bill, you know that. I just don't want you bringing that disease up in here."

Bill washed his hands, using his kerchief as a washcloth. He washed his face and hands, right up to the elbows, working the homemade disinfectant into every pore of his skin. She threw him out a cotton flannel to dry himself with. He crossed the threshold, and they embraced. He smelt of lavender now. Lavender and the rest.

"Bill, there's something I have to tell you. I think we should move north, try to outrun this disease."

"North? You mean to Canada? To your parents?"

She hesitated. "Yes. I think if we get across the border...."

"Now Carol, in all these years that I've known you, you've never wanted to go back North. You never tell me anything about your parents – always been so darn secretive. And your little ways...I've always appreciated your ways, but now they're worse than ever. Sometimes I think you want me to spin around thrice and do a jig before you let me into the house."

Carol looked away, her eyes drawn to the loose floorboard concealing her sewing kit. It had been twenty years since she had started this expedition. She was supposed to return after three to present her findings, link in with the university and give her initial report. Get more OCD medication.

She had made the worst mistake any cultural anthropologist could make. Gone Native. Lost, submerged in her work, sleeping with her subjects! If she went back, she would be dismissed from her post – and she would not be allowed to return, would never see Bill again. But, in the face of this sickness, going home might be their only option for survival.

"What's for breakfast anyway?" asked Bill, changing the subject. Carol put a second pot on the stove, smaller than the first but more worn. She must have scrubbed that pot ten thousand times. The stove was still hot, so she added oats to water and stirred. Not long later, they were both enjoying porridge and honey. They ate in silence.

Carol thought about the potential journey. Not much would have changed since then: they could follow the Hudson River out of New York, pass the lakes through Vermont and on towards Quebec. It was maybe three hundred miles.

Carol was cataloguing what they would take. They had two horses: Bill's big stallion and her smaller mare. They had their wagon, which would comfortably take two, plus modest supplies for two weeks' travel. They had a couple of sacks of oats, five Mason jars of pickled vegetables from last year, a barrel of potatoes, Bill's bowie knife, bow, quiver, her sewing kit, blankets....

Bill coughed. "Just clearing my throat," he explained. Recently, every time anyone coughed, they felt the need to explain why.

They went to bed early that night. She added kerosene lamps to her mental list. *I should tell him,* she thought. Matches. Wax candles. The metal lunch box. She couldn't forget that.

Bill was late getting out of bed the next morning. Probably just tired from the long ride in and out of town yesterday, so she let him sleep in. While she waited for him to wake, she went out to feed and water the horses. Their paddock had the best view of their homestead: their log cabin, three rooms, an outhouse, easy access to the river, an allotment for growing vegetables. Each vegetable grown in its own section, planted in straight lines. Would she give it all up? She would torch it to the ground if it meant she would get to live an extra moment with Bill.

Carol took a spade and went out to the oak tree. Three feet south and west of the trunk as it faced the house, she dug until she hit a metal lunch box. She wrapped it in cheesecloth and hid it from her husband in her basket.

By the time she had returned to the kitchen, Bill was up and about. He was stiff, she could tell. He was making coffee: grounds brewed in a tin.

"We can't leave this place, Carol. The town needs you," he spoke into the coffee tin.

Carol knew this to be true. She was the midwife, herbalist, wise woman, and confidant to half the town. Reluctant in the role and refusing to be engaged formally. She had never trained anyone to replace her, though there were countless applicants and over the years, a couple even capable. It would be a step too far. She would be disrupting the development of their society, accelerating their medical and scientific knowledge unfairly.

"Bill, this sickness is different to the others."

He turned and faced her. Flashed his full toothy smile and bright blue eyes. "You'll find something to fix it, Carol. You always do. I ain't seen a fever you can't cool down."

Over the years, she had sparingly used what medical supplies she had brought with her, unbeknownst to the village. A little penicillin added to a broth to help with an infection or ground up paracetamol in a tea when there was severe pain.

Her anthropologist side found it interesting. Scientific development and understanding were relatively equivalent between this era and the 1600s, yet nobody had accused her of being a witch. This was perhaps, she hypothesised, as there was no formal religion in New America. Or perhaps, no strict patriarchy like the 1600s.

Carol began to cry. At first, she cried slow, wet tears, then the shuddering wail of a lifetime of anxiety burst from her lips. *He'll never know, and I can't tell him*, she thought.

He closed the distance and held her to his chest as she sobbed. Wholesome Bill, a man of many actions and few words. Her tears made him feel guilty, she thought. If only he knew she had been lying to him all these years.

She broke off and left the kitchen, leaving Bill standing there, bewildered. She fed the hens and collected eggs. She chopped wood until her arms ached. Stacked the logs in piles of two and three, never single or groups of four. Carol counted and then recounted the tins of beans she had stockpiled, inspecting all for spoilage, making sure each label faced outwards in a nice pattern. It was only three hundred miles away. A week's riding, ten days...two weeks if it was bad. Plenty of time to talk and explain. To make him understand.

More sounds of horses and wagons. Jennifer Marbury and her husband, Tom. A friendly sight up until the sickness. Carol would consider Jennifer a friend; she'd attended her three births. Tom was a reliable man who washed his hands and didn't beat his wife. That made him one of the best in the town. Carol knew what they wanted from the moment she saw their faces, and she also knew in that moment that she couldn't help. She was back inside before they had alighted from their carriage. Tom carried little Alice in his arms.

"Hold it right there, Tom," Carol called as soon as Tom was in earshot.

"Come on, Carol." Bill came up behind her and pleaded, so only she could hear. "Since when do we refuse good neighbours our hospitality? They need help."

"Shush Bill, this is different," Carol snapped. She turned back to the unwelcome visitors. "Jennifer, Tom, I know why you're here. And it breaks my heart to see baby Alice this way. But there's nothing I can do for you. There's nothing I can do to stop this sickness or ease its passing. It's a contagion. If you come any closer, you'll risk myself and Bill. And I can't allow that." The words came out strong and true, the hint of a threat hanging heavy in the air.

At first, she thought the sickness was a bacterial infection of some sort, something that might respond to her secret stash of antibiotics. Then she hoped it was a relatively mild but self-limiting virus, something you got over if you were healthy and strong. But people got real sick, real quickly, and she knew there was nothing in her supplies for it. She had been vaccinated in the university hospital in her youth with one of those wonder vaccines created in the immunology golden age of the 2020s. They cured the common cold! She was likely immune, as she had been exposed in the early days to almost everyone sick in the village. It was Bill she was trying to protect.

"Those boils on your hands, Tom, are the first signs of infection. You're strong, as are your wife and your three children. You have as good a chance as anyone else at beating this, but there's nothing I can do to improve the odds. I know you think I've got some secret healing powers up here, but that's not the truth. This isn't like pneumonia; there's no special brew for it. You let this take its course at home, where you can't put anyone else in danger. Keep yourself fed and drink plenty of water." She didn't let them speak, left no pause in the conversation enough for them to reply. She was firm and clear. She kept her gaze locked, but her thoughts were pulled towards the metal lunch boxed buried beneath the oak tree.

Jennifer and Tom, some of her closest acquaintances, got back in their wagon and rode away. Jennifer's shoulders were shaking, and Alice was moaning. Tom's face was set and fierce with betrayal. Carol knew she would never see them again, even if, by blind luck, they survived.

"That was cold, Carol. That was cold and mean," Bill said.

"I know, Bill. I know. Get the wagon; we're going today."

"Hold it just one darn second. I ain't going anywhere until I know where and why."

Bill was obviously a lot more connected to the town and to the house than she was. He had lived his entire forty-three years here. Bill's parents had lived here, died here. Once, Carol had estimated that Bill had probably met fewer than three hundred people in his entire life and that he probably knew fewer than thirty on a first-name basis. Everything and everyone he knew was based within twenty-five kilometres of where they were standing. Carol estimated Bill's Great-Grandfather would have been a child when the war ended.

Carol took Bill's hands in hers and looked him in the eye.

"There is nothing left for us in this town, Bill. Sooner or later, the sickness will come for us. We can move somewhere, try to outrun it, but I fear if it's made it here, it's probably following trade lines. And you know as well as I Canada does not trade with America, so Canada is our best bet. My parents are still alive, Bill – well, at least, I *hope* they are. I can get us over the border. You just have to trust me, just one last time. Please, Bill."

Bill said nothing for a long moment. Then, to Carol's relief, he nodded.

There were a few things Carol could not leave behind: her journal, her lunch box from beneath the oak tree, the sewing kit from under the loose floorboard. They loaded the wagon with the essential supplies and prepared to say goodbye to their perfect little homestead in Albany, New York.

While Bill was out back with the horses, Carol opened the sewing kit, released the secret clasp, and retrieved the GPS navigation tool. It was military grade and solar-powered. Like Hansel and Gretel, Carol had left crumbs she could follow along the way that would give off a little signal. She set it to vibrate only.

The journey was longer than she had expected but more comfortable, too. The wagon, with its waxy tarpaulin, was their shelter both from the sun during the day and the cold at night. They took the dirt roads north, which eventually turned to trails. They abandoned the wagon there and went on horseback for a bit, the GPS vibrating a little more frequently as they went along. When the trails gave way to tracks, they released the horses and completed the rest on foot. Carol could recognise some of the route; she pretended it was the river that was guiding her, but she would have been lost without the GPS.

While Bill was off gathering firewood for their first camp in the open air, Carol unwrapped the cheesecloth from around the lunch box and opened its rusted metal clasps. She took out the resealable polyethylene bag; the plastic felt foreign on her fingers. From this, she shook out another parcel: aluminium mylar she had first sealed together twenty years ago. She tipped the contents out onto the plastic bag.

"What you got there, sport?" Bill asked.

Springs, a screwdriver, pliers, a non-descript metal or polymer parts, all coated in a wax. A magazine, sights, barrel and the other characteristic components of an antique handgun. Bill took in the scene and was dumbfounded. It took Carol a moment to make something up.

"Oh…this is just a device I need to put together to be able to find my way home."

Bill picked up a can of spraying lubricant oil and examined it, confusion in every line of his face.

"Look, I'll show you." Carol prised the can from his hands and sprayed down the metallic parts, then wiped off the excess. There were some laminated instructions for reassembly. Carol had done this once a year for the last twenty years and practised it one hundred times before that. It was nice to keep the instructions, though. The assembly was done in silence, slowly and surely cleaned and reassembled the handgun, a Glock 9mm. Carol loaded ten rounds into the magazine and clicked it into place, pulled the slide and loaded a round into the chamber. She released the magazine, pumped the slide again and caught the released bullet in her palm.

Then she put everything back in the lunch box without further comment.

"Carol, I think it's about time you got some things off your chest."

Carol froze.

The silence was interpreted by a rustling and then

a low-pitched growl. Bill mouthed the word 'bear', and Carol nodded. He took his hunting bow and nocked an arrow. Carol followed Bill's lead: he had already spotted the bear and was aiming.

Carol stood beside Bill, preparing to shoot. There was no outrunning or hiding from a grizzly bear here. The grizzly moved out of the forest and into the clearing towards camp. There wasn't much food about, but it must have caught the scent of something, maybe the horses, maybe herself and Bill.

Bill started talking, slowly and gently first. "I know you know we're here bear, you can smell us better than we can see you. We don't want no trouble."

Bill and Carol sidestepped towards higher ground, moving like dance partners. Carol knew her small handgun would not necessarily kill a bear, certainly not on the first try. She didn't particularly trust her aim or the reliability of a gun buried for twenty years. However, this was the type of emergency she had brought it for. She found a moment of solace in the fact it was a bear rather than Tom Marbery she was about to aim it at.

The bear looked at them and back to the camp. Carol had left most of her stuff at the campsite and would shoot in order to retrieve it. It was essential for her re-entry into Canada. She hoped the bear would lose interest and wander off itself. There were fifteen metres between them. While Bill had an excellent shot, that bow was useful for killing deer and small game – not necessarily for taking out bears.

Bill was side-on to the bear now and had a good shot at the heart.

"You shoot first, Bill."

He let the arrow fly, and the bear roared. Carol squeezed the trigger. The sound and the recoil shocked her, despite her best intentions. She fell backwards, and the bear charged. It was almost upon her when she released four more rounds, at least two into the head. It collapsed, dead.

It was over in a matter of seconds. Adrenaline pumping through her body, she felt dizzy, uncertain. She looked over at Bill, who was on the ground. The wave of anxiety coursing through her turned to dread.

"Bill! Bill, are you okay?"

He turned. He was alive. "What was that? What made that awful sound?"

"It was a gun, Bill; it was my gun."

"What in hell's name is a gun, Carol?"

She wanted to tell him everything, to tell him the truth. How, almost one hundred years ago, there had been a second American civil war. Millions of deaths. Almost the rest of the entire world joining together to nullify the American nuclear threat. International embargoes on transport, trade, and technology. America set back into pre-industrial times.

But not now. Not yet. They needed to move. She raced around their campsite, gathering only what was essential and stuffing it into a burlap sack. Anyone could have heard that gunshot. Guns were banned, even antique ones. She had also killed a grizzly bear, possibly part of some ecological study.

"Bill, please, I promise I'll tell you everything soon." She wanted to get to the Canadian border. She took the GPS out of her pocket, averting her eyes from Bill's burning stare. "We can't camp here, but the lake is only a kilometre away. Let's trek there and set up camp. I know somewhere."

They marched in silence. They came across the remnants of Lake Champlain bridge. It was old. Only the bases remained, as the arch had broken away. But, despite its dilapidated state, it was an excellent landmark, and Carol was able to find the emergency cabin located on the south-east bank. Carol opened her lunch box and took the oil spray, and found the key in her sewing kit. After a little greasing, the lock opened. Under the light of a lit wax candle, she found the emergency generator and activated it. She flicked the light switch: electricity, for the first time in twenty years!

"Damn it, Carol, what the hell is going on?! What is this?!" Bill was blinded by the lights, staring in wide-eyed horror at the woman he thought he knew.

"I'm sorry Bill. It's – it's hard to know where to begin…." When she plucked up the courage to look him in the eye, she realised Bill was no longer in the cabin. She rushed outside: he was standing near the lake. "Bill, Bill, wait!"

By the time she had joined him, a loud sound ricocheted across the lake. In the distance, she could make out a tactical helicopter swooping across the skies.

Bill's mouth opened and closed.

"Bill, listen to me. Put down that bow. Don't say anything, and *don't* move." Carol knew if the Canadian authorities suspected Americans had discovered a weapons cache, the International Treaty allowed them to take immediate action to nullify the threat.

The helicopter created an awful racket, and she knew it was no use trying to speak further. She opened up her sewing kit and shook the contents onto the ground before releasing the catch to the hidden compartment. She took out her passport and credentials.

The helicopter landed on the lake and taxied up to the shore. Carol could see the pilot, co-pilot and two others in the back holding assault weapons. The armed soldiers alighted. She held her ground. They were dressed in blue military uniforms with helmets and face masks.

"Bill, please, you don't need to do anything. I will explain as soon as I can. I love you."

When the men with the rifles were close enough that the noise of the rotatory blades wouldn't drown her out, she announced:

"Je suis un citoyen Canadien. Je m'appelle Carol Archambault. Je suis professor d'anthropologie en

Université de Montréal. Mes documents requis." She offered her passport and identification to the soldiers. "Je demande l'asile politique pour cet homme."

The soldiers took her documents and returned to the helicopter, presumably to discuss it with their superiors in the Quebec ministry.

"Bill, I know this all must be strange to you —"

"So, the stories are true?"

"What stories, Bill?"

"That we once lived in the sky and flew on ships and killed each other?"

"I'll explain later, Bill."

# THE ASYLUM SEEKER

## Pierce Grace

Dr John Browne was sitting in his office in the Lunatic Asylum reading his newspaper. He was shaking his head at the news of the disturbances around the country and wondered where it would all end. Lloyd George's world 'fit for heroes' didn't seem to be developing terribly well, especially in Ireland. Everything had certainly changed with the war and people seemed discontented in their lives. There was a general feeling of unease about. A knock on the door brought him back from his reverie.

"Come in," he said.

Martin Fitzpatrick's head appeared around the door. "Sorry for disturbing you, doctor, but we have had a phone call from the R.I.C. They want to bring a prisoner to us."

"Oh yes, what seems to be the matter with him?" asked Dr Browne.

"Well, it seems he is a bit soft-in-the-head, sir," Fitzpatrick said casually.

Dr Browne exploded with annoyance. "Soft-in-the-head! Really, Fitzpatrick, you are the most senior charge attendant in this asylum, and the best you can come up with is 'soft-in-the-head'. You know that since Dr Freud's work in Vienna, psychological medicine is advancing in leaps and bounds, and I am sure that in ten years' time, we will have made significant progress in treating these patients. Patients, Fitzpatrick! Not lunatics or soft-in-the-head-atics! I expect by 1930, we will not use the word lunatic at all! Sometimes I despair of bringing any modern ideas into this institution." Dr Browne shook his head again. He seemed to be doing a lot of that lately.

"Yes sir, sorry sir," Fitzpatrick replied. "It's just that Dr Leahy, who was here before you as the R.M.S. used to see our role more as wardens rather than curers. He used to say we are here 'to protect the public, treat the lunatics humanely and keep them under lock and key for their own good'. It's difficult to get used to new ideas. Anyway, the prisoner is on his way with two constables, so they should be here shortly."

"All right. All right". Dr Browne said as he calmed down. He had this conversation many times before, and he felt guilty for losing his temper with Fitzpatrick, who really was an excellent 'charge'. "I am going to my quarters to see my little daughter before she

goes to bed. Let me know when he gets here," Dr Browne said.

He was always amused at the phrase 'quarters'

used in reference to the apartments set aside for the Resident Medical Superintendent in the asylum. If he had a quarter of the asylum, he would have had more rooms than the Grand Hotel in Tramore, where he often went on holidays.

Later that evening, Dr Browne was called to see the prisoner or patient, depending on one's point of view. An unkempt, tired-looking young man was standing in the middle of the admission ward with his arms extended. He seemed quiet and lost in thought. Fitzpatrick and another attendant were trying to talk to him, but to no avail. The two young constables of the Royal Irish Constabulary who had brought him to the asylum were intrigued as to what was going to happen to their ex-prisoner. They had heard stories of straitjackets and padded cells and were willing to help if a bit of manhandling was required.

"What is your name, son?" Dr Browne asked gently.

"I am the way, the truth and the light, I am the Lord thy God, the creator of worlds and the fount of knowledge. Love me, and you will be saved; hate me, and you will be damned!" the young man said to no one in particular.

"Yes, of course you are," said Dr Browne. Then under his breath, "You and all the others who think they are God. But where do you come from?"

Loudly, the young man declaimed: "I am not 'from', I 'am', now, always was, and always will be forever and ever, Amen." He finished by turning his hands towards the ceiling as in supplication, looking upwards.

"Yes. Amen to that," said Dr Browne. "Are you not tired, holding your arms out like that?" he asked.

"I am the alpha and the omega, the destroyer of worlds, the giver of life, God the Father, Son and Holy Ghost," the young man continued, as though he had heard nothing.

Dr Browne turned to Fitzpatrick and said: "Oh well, we are not going to get very far with him tonight. Take him to the observation ward and see if he will eat something. Our friends in the Royal Irish Constabulary are not known for their generous hospitality. I expect the poor fellow is starving. He will probably fall asleep after a while. Catatonia is very tiring, you know. At least he is not violent like the last fellow they brought us. However, please tell the ward attendant to have some chloral hydrate standing by just in case and get me if he acts up."

After the young man was taken away Dr Browne asked Fitzpatrick, "Do you know where they found him?"

"Well, sir, you know there was a terrible ambush downtown two days ago?"

Dr Browne nodded again; he had heard that two soldiers from the Devonshire Regiment had died in the attack.

Fitzpatrick continued quietly so that the

constables wouldn't hear. "A patrol of Tommies bringing provisions to the gaol was attacked, and two of the soldiers were killed. The usual rounding up followed with the Black and Tans going berserk after a heavy night's drinking in their depot. They rounded up loads of people but thank God they didn't kill anyone; just the usual blackguarding, wild shooting, wrecking houses, and driving people off the road in the Crossley tenders. This poor lad was standing doing an imitation of the crucified Christ on the Wexford road. The Tans put him in the tender and made a terrible mockery of him; those heathens told him that they really would crucify him when they got him back to the depot."

"Oh! How dreadful. The Tans are nothing better than savages," commented Dr Browne with another little shake of his head.

"Fortunately," Fitzpatrick continued, "because it was nearer, they brought him to the military barracks in town rather than to their own depot, which is fifteen miles away in an old mansion out in the country. If he had gone there, he would be dead now. Colonel Knox, the commanding officer at the military barracks, a decent man by all accounts, happened to be present when the Tans brought our friend in and could see the fellow was not right in the head."

Dr Browne was about to say something when Fitzpatrick quickly corrected himself, "Sorry, I mean 'very disturbed', sir."

Dr Browne nodded. "Yes, I know of Colonel Knox, and he is said to be a fair man."

Fitzpatrick continued with the story. "The colonel ordered him put in the cells for observation. The young lad stood there for five hours with his arms extended, telling them all to repent or be damned. He also said he knew they were sending him messages through the telephone. Eventually, Knox felt that his prisoner was genuinely mad, sorry, disturbed, and had the army doctor examine him. The medical officer, Captain O'Sullivan, took one look at him and ordered that he be brought to the asylum immediately, and that's what happened. As the R.I.C. is usually responsible for accompanying disturbed prisoners to the asylum, Colonel Knox asked them to provide two constables to escort our man, which they did."

"Poor fellow. He must have been frightened out of his wits," Dr Browne said, shaking his head again. He continued in a brighter mood, 'You seem to be very well informed, Fitzpatrick. Well done. There is nothing like getting a good history, either direct or collateral, to get to the bottom of a medical problem. There's hope yet that we will bring modern medicine to bear on these problems of the mind. Well done again. You handled this problem extremely well."

"Why, thank you, doctor," Fitzpatrick replied.

"I am off to bed now," said Dr Browne. "Let me know if there is a problem. Good night, well done again." With that, Dr Browne headed off back to his

'Grand Hotel' feeling very pleased with the way his staff had dealt with the admission.

"Good night, sir," replied Fitzpatrick, smiling to himself.

The next morning, Dr Browne was in his office early after a good night's sleep. He greeted his charge attendant cheerily, "Good morning Fitzpatrick, how are you today?"

"Very well, doctor, thank you."

"I thought I heard a bit of a commotion in the night, but as no one came to get me, I fell asleep again. I hope everything is well."

"Very well, sir, yes, very well," Fitzpatrick replied, smiling.

"Oh, by the way, how is that poor chap who was admitted last night?" asked Doctor Browne.

Matter-of-factly, Fitzpatrick said, "Oh, he's gone, sir."

Dr Browne could hardly believe what he had heard. "Gone! What do you mean, he's gone? Patients don't just walk out of asylums. They have to be discharged."

"I know that, sir," Fitzpatrick replied, "but as they had guns, we didn't dispute the matter with them."

"They? Dispute? Guns? What are you talking about, Fitzpatrick?" asked Dr Browne, who couldn't understand how a seriously ill patient had just left the asylum and nobody stopped him.

Fitzpatrick patiently explained what had happened.

"Well, shortly after the R.I.C. constables left, a number of armed men came in a lorry to collect him. They were from an IRA flying column, and a tough-looking lot they were too. They said, 'we have no quarrel with anyone here. We just want to take Jimmy away with us.'"

Incredulous, Dr Browne, shaking his head again, asked, "How did they know he was here or that the police weren't still here? My God, if the police had left an armed guard, like they did before, we could have had a shoot-out in the hospital. It doesn't bear thinking about. How did they get in, for goodness' sake? The gates are locked every night at eight o'clock."

"Best not ask, sir," Fitzpatrick said firmly.

Dr Browne still couldn't believe what he was hearing. "Did they take him away? Who arranged it all?"

"He did, sir. Jimmy did."

"Jimmy? Was that his real name? But Jimmy was a mad as a hatter. He couldn't organise...." Dr Browne's voice trailed off as he began to realise what had happened.

"Mad as a hatter, sir?" Fitzpatrick asked quizzically.

"Well, I mean very disturbed, of course," Dr Browne corrected himself. "But obviously, he wasn't psychotic at all. Was he involved in the ambush?"

"I believe he planned it, sir," Fitzpatrick said.

"Really? He must be a high-up in the IRA then."

"Very high up."

"How did he end up on the Wexford road?"

Fitzpatrick went into explaining mode again. "Well, you see, Dr Browne, after the ambush, the column scattered in different directions, and Jimmy was making his way along the Wexford road when he saw the Tans coming. They were on him before he could get out of the way. He adopted the pose of a catatonic and started babbling about God and religion. You know the rest."

Dr Browne was puzzled as to how a country boy could pull off such a stunt so well. Giving voice to his thoughts, he said, "But he did it brilliantly. He even had me fooled, and I am an experienced psychiatrist. I wonder where he learned about schizophrenia or who coached him."

"I couldn't say, sir," Fitzpatrick offered.

Frowning, Dr Browne continued, "I wonder, was it Captain O'Sullivan, the army doctor? He is a dark horse, you know, but I suspect he has strong republican sympathies. It's a wonder he ever became an army doctor, but I suppose it was because of the war. Lots of my old colleagues joined the Royal Army Medical Corps."

"Yes, sir," said Fitzpatrick. "He was with the Leinsters in Flanders. He had a terrible time of it, but apparently won the Military Cross and was well-liked by the men. He took great care of the wounded, but he was shocked at what happened after 1916 in Dublin."

"Yes, yes, as we all were," said Dr Browne, nodding his head for a change. "Do you know Jimmy's last name or is that best not to know too?"

"Oh! No, sir, his name is Jimmy Fitzpatrick," replied the charge attendant.

Dr Browne, not certain that he wanted to know the answer, said, "That's your name, Fitzpatrick. Is he by any chance…?"

"Yes, sir. He's Jimmy. He is my younger brother, sir," Fitzpatrick replied proudly. "Dr O'Sullivan looked after him in Flanders and is still looking out for him. He recognised him the minute he laid eyes on him in the barracks."

"Ah, I see it all now," said Dr Browne. "In that case, Fitzpatrick, I suppose we need not be in any rush in letting the authorities know that our absconder, whoever he was, has left us for alternative accommodation."

"No, sir. Thank you, sir," replied Fitzpatrick with a grin.

"Now I had best get on with my rounds". Dr Browne was shaking his head as he went down the long corridor towards the male wards. How on earth was he going to explain this to the Management Committee?

# THE ROAD TO BOULDER

Frank McKenna

The sun cindered in the rear-view mirror as they reached the peak, tinting the dust and the tawny grass. The earth unfolded before them. The only evidence of humanity was the road, which wove in and out of view, winding down the mountain and reaching out to the horizon.

Tucker was telling Henry about a place in Boulder where you could rent inflatable rings and ride them down the river.

"We're not kids," Henry sighed, tugging his sleeves over his hands.

"It's supposed to be fun. Worth doing. If it's no good, we'll find something else and do that. Life is going to be different, Henry. I mean, look at this." He swept a panoramic hand across the windscreen.

"Look at what?"

"I'm going to paint this. Once we're settled, I'm going to drive back up here and sit with my kit and put it all on the canvas. I'll spend days at it. *Weeks,* if

I have to. There's something to find here, Henry. No buildings or streets. No nine-to-five or dickhead bosses or fuckhead customers. Just vast beauty."

That's when they ran out of gas.

The engine cutting out left silence and a sense of floating, like the moment after the last click of a roller-coaster's chains as it tips over the highest point of its rail.

Tucker pulled over and fiddled with the key, hoping the car might reignite on a shifting dreg of fuel. "I'm sorry," he said.

"We should have stopped for gas."

Tucker stared into the steering wheel. "It was a hundred miles ago," he said.

"Yes. And the sign said: *No gas for 126 miles.*" Henry tapped on his phone and swiped away the notifications. Eight missed calls. Eleven messages. Google Maps took a few seconds to open, seconds more before it allowed him to type.

"Nothing," he said. "No internet. No GPS."

"Phone signal?"

Henry shook his head.

They roved their eyes over the hundreds of square miles before them, over the shifts in colour that followed terrain changes. No boundaries. No markings. Just the sky rolling over the land.

"We'll have to stop the next car," said Tucker.

"We haven't seen a car since that fucking gas station we didn't go into."

Tucker pressed out slow breaths, counting silent numbers. Out for four seconds, in for four seconds, out for four, in for four....

"I wouldn't bother," said Henry. "None of that stuff works." He craned his head over the dash. "You see that?"

A bird was carving an arc not far in front, just above their eye line.

"An eagle?"

"I don't know," said Henry. "Big fucking bird."

They watched the creature skim across the sky. It ignored their box of metal and rode the air, stretching into its span and surveying the mountainside and the miles beyond.

"A vulture, maybe?" asked Tucker.

"Waiting for a couple of idiots to run out of gas."

They watched the bird until its silhouette was lost behind them in the sinking sun. Then they sat for a moment, perched high on the mountain, perhaps on a slight downslope, until Tucker wondered if power in the engine might not be immediately necessary.

He released the brake.

A moment later, stones snapped under the tyres, and the car eased forward. "Ha!" He steered them back onto the tarmac. The snapping stopped, and the car found its rhythm on the smoother surface.

They were moving again.

Over about five minutes of powerless downhill cruising, their descent was overtaken by the mountain's lengthening shadow. Tucker turned on the headlights.

"We might make it," he said, his leg jiggling with excitement.

"I'm not sure that being stranded at the bottom is any better than being stranded at the top."

"We're still moving," said Tucker. "We just need to keep moving."

"The great rescue continues."

"I had to do something," Tucker snapped, glancing at Henry's wrists.

The sleeves had ridden up again. The bandages were still crisp and taught. No fraying yet on the edges. Still pulling at the hairs on his forearms.

"We did what we were supposed to do," said Tucker. "Ask for help. Isn't that what those fucking ads say? They don't tell you that the help isn't worth shit."

"It wasn't their fault."

"Breathing exercises? A thought diary? It's fucking baby shit. It's fucking paint-by-numbers bullshit."

Henry stared through the window on his side. "I didn't always do it," he said. He curled up, pulling his knees to his chest. "I didn't always take the meds, either."

"You went to all the appointments. Every single one. For two years. Psychiatrists. Psychologists. Nurses. And it got worse and worse. They haven't a clue what they're doing. No. We had to get away."

Henry tried to turn on the heat.

"Car's off," Tucker reminded him. "You want to get a coat from the back?"

"Better not stop. Just in case."

Below, headlights rounded a corner and turned to face them. An oncoming vehicle. Henry clapped and thumped Tucker on the shoulder.

"Told you we'd be all right, bro!"

Tucker looked at the speedometer. The needle was stuck below zero. They were tipping along, though, maybe forty or fifty. "You want to stop them?" he asked.

"Yes, Tucker, I do."

Tucker strained to see beyond the oncoming headlights, beyond the mountain at the road that reached out until it reached the sky.

"We could just...keep going," he said. "We have, you know, momentum."

"Momentum? We're rolling down a mountain! Pull over."

Tucker squeezed on the brake and they slowed, but then he released again and the car sped up.

"We don't need help, Henry," he said.

"Oh, God."

"Come on. We're going to be fine. We've had enough of asking people for help."

Henry tried to honk the horn, but it made no sound. The car shook as a dusty black Dodge rattled by. The driver, lit up in the clash of lights, raised a salutary hand as he passed.

Henry gently hit his head against the dash.

Miles further, the evening setting in, a shadow broke the line of the road ahead. The closer they got, the clearer the shape of a crouched figure formed. Long and thin, the creature craned its head towards them. Its round, bright yellow eyes sat above a hooked beak. It was a bird – perhaps what they'd seen circling in the sky. It stood taller as they approached, as tall as the car. It was standing over a carcass – something open and dog-like.

The bird didn't move. Once their headlights passed, it was in shadow again, but the car rolled by only feet away and Henry and the bird stared into each other, neither flinching, both prepared for who-knows-what.

"Fucking hell," whistled Tucker, once the bird returned attention to its feed. "He didn't even blink!"

A few miles further, they rounded a bend, and the road began to incline. The car slowed, and slowed further, until it stopped.

"Bit of an anti-climax," said Henry.

"What are we going to do?"

Henry tapped the screen on his phone. "Nothing," he said. "There's nothing we can do. It was a nice idea, that life might be better in the merry old land of Boulder."

"Stop it."

"Seriously. It was a nice idea – you quitting your shitty job, thinking I was going to get inspired or something." He peered into the darkness ahead. "There's no wisdom out there, Tucker. If we get out of this car, we're just two pricks with shitty lives standing in the dark in a place we don't belong. Vast beauty? All that means is big and empty."

"Stop!" Tucker shouted. "Stop being so fucking selfish. You think these two years have been easy for me?"

It took a few seconds for Henry to hook words on his breath. "I know," he said. "I'm sorry."

"I'm sick of sorry. Do you know what I'd be doing now if you'd fucking died? I'd be comforting our mother. I'd be getting cramps in my arms from trying to keep the life squeezed into her."

Tucker turned off the lights, and they sat in a partial night-sky glow. "We've got jumpers and coats," he said. "We can push off the road and wrap up for the night. Something will come by in the morning."

"Then on to Boulder."

"Yeah, well, I didn't hear any ideas coming from you."

They sat and stared through the windscreen and out over the darkened land beneath. Nothing shifted. There was nothing but the air and the land, waiting.

"I know Boulder is a stupid idea," said Tucker, after a while.

Henry traced a finger over the bandage on his left

wrist, over the line of the wound. "Not the worst idea I've heard recently."

"I know where you are doesn't change anything. 'The best place to live in the world'. I know they just make those lists up. Just pluck them out of the air. I know that. But I was desperate." He looked at his brother. "I thought we were in it together," he said.

Henry slowly lifted his head. He had not met his brother's eyes since the other night, since he took the blade to his wrists. Since long before that, if he was honest.

He had let Tucker bring him to the appointments. He had given his consent for Tucker to speak to the doctors, to hear of his despairing mood and his dark thoughts. He had shared with Tucker the homework and the worksheets, and Tucker had gone through them with him. Good old Tucker didn't act as the cheerleader or the whip-cracker. He got right in beside Henry and tried out all the gimmicks. And managed not to be condescending about it, like they were really in it together.

But Henry couldn't look him in the eye because then Tucker would see the truth. And if he saw the truth, Tucker would have known there was no point in any of it. Henry couldn't crush his brother's hope, not when it was the thing that made Tucker more alive than Henry could ever be.

Henry was an absence. A non-person. That's why none of it could work. It wasn't the doctors' fault. It wasn't Tucker's. It wasn't even his. There was no gas to ignite, and he was exhausted, rolling along, hoping nobody would notice the silence.

He looked at his brother and allowed Tucker to meet his eyes. There was an immense and predictable urge to flee – to yank on the door handle and burst into the night air and the wilderness. But he stayed, waited on the urge to shrivel away, waited to be seen, to be unmasked. For the truth to dawn on his brother, and for that to be it.

Henry's eyes filled with tears. His whole body felt full of them.

"So," said Tucker, wiping his own watering eyes. "Should we get the coats from the back?"

Henry blinked. Then he looked at the road ahead.

"No," he said, putting a hand on his brother's arm. "You stay." He opened the passenger door and moved to the boot of the car.

"What are you doing?"

"Keep off the brakes!" Henry shouted.

He planted his hands on the back of the car and bent his knees. Tension gathered in his thighs. As they filled, it was like they were being wrung. Flames built inside them. He roared, wringing them more.

When he overcame the friction between tyres and road, the car jolted forward. It inched up the incline, rolling back if he let up. The wounds on his wrists throbbed. He stepped and breathed loudly through gritted teeth. Six or seven steps in, the car rolled easier. He quickened to a slow-motion jog.

But by the time he heard Tucker call his name, he had worked up to a full-on run. He lifted his head to see over the roof of the car but saw only darkness lit up.

Tucker called again.

Henry dipped his hips and straightened the line of his body, his head face-down between his extended arms. He sent every step, every press-off through the car.

Then the car was gone from his hands.

He fell forward, face-planting into the road. For a moment, there was only pain. His face, his wrists. He was sure the stitches had opened; he could feel blood seeping and the bandages moistening.

The red tail-lights moved quickly downhill in front. Then the car screeched and careened to a stop diagonally across the road.

Henry checked his nose for tenderness and for blood – there was both.

Tucker ran back, pulled Henry to his feet, and held him up by the shoulders. He wiped Henry's face with his sleeve and aided him back to the car, his arm around Henry's shoulders.

They set off again.

The slope was steep. Tucker had to keep a squeeze on the brake to stay on the road going around the bends.

Soon they came to the bottom of the mountain. Tucker let off the brake from a few hundred metres out and they sped into it, the car rattling and squeaking. Both men bounced in their seats.

"Go, go, go!" shouted Henry. He meant it. He wanted to ramp into the straight. He wanted to feel them take off.

The speed pared off slowly once the road flattened.

About two miles after shooting off the bottom – about twenty from where they had run out of gas at the top – they crossed a lip in the road, descended into a hollow and rounded an easy bend. There, their faces and the inside of the car lit up in the glow of a red gas station canopy.

They shouted and grabbed each other's shirts and shook each other as Tucker guided the car to a pump. He pulled the hand brake, and the brothers hugged.

Outside, Henry took the gas nozzle. "You go in and pay," he told his brother. "I'll look after the gas from now on."

He watched Tucker walk towards the station. The inside was pale and bright. He could see a girl through the window, maybe in her twenties. She had long, brown hair pulled into a tight ponytail that reached down her back. She got up from a stool behind the counter and unfurled her slouch as Tucker approached the glass door.

From where Henry was, the mountain's shoulders

lurked above and around the crest of the station's hollow. Then he looked in the other direction, where Boulder must be, a couple of hours away. Above the road, above the shadowed terrain, the sky was a brilliant navy canvas, set alight by stars and a crescent moon.

# DID YOU ENJOY THESE STORIES? YOU CAN HELP US!

We are proud of our work, and honest reviews can help bring this collection to the attention of other readers. If you've enjoyed it, we would be very grateful if you could spend a few minutes leaving a review on your preferred online store. It can be as short or long as you like!

# ABOUT THE AUTHORS

Henry O'Connell works as a consultant psychiatrist in Portlaoise and as a Clinical Professor with the University of Limerick School of Medicine. He has always dabbled in creative writing, never until now thinking that he would see his ramblings appearing outside of his own laptop. He lives in his native Ballina, Co. Tipperary with his wife Kathy and children Sophie, Isabelle and Henry.

***

Frank McKenna is a writer and trainee psychiatrist. Winner of the Michael Mullan Cancer Fund Short Story Competition 2018, he subscribes to the wisdom that stories help us understand the world, and has embarked on the foolhardy quest of trying to tell them.

***

Kevin Lally is a trainee psychiatrist living in the Midwest of Ireland. Despite four university degrees, two university diplomas and two college memberships, his Everest remains the driving test, thus proving that, with enough creativity, procrastination and avoidance, any molehill can be turned into a mountain.

Printed in Great Britain
by Amazon